Noble Shadows

A Novel by William Clark

The moral right of the author has been asserted.

The characters and events portrayed in this book are fictitious. Any similarity to real person, living or dead, is coincidental and not intended by the author.

Content

Forward

At sixty-one, I now see things for what they really are: a cosmic crapshoot where the house has rigged most of the games we play. The lives we live seem to be for the entertainment of the main shot-caller. Sadly, we were made to think we were in control of the dice. But not a chance, buckaroo; the house always wins. It is a sobering realization at any age.

This writing thing that I do, this game I am playing for all it's worth, will be the end of the line for me. It is my last great crusade in the battle to rise above stunning mediocrity. This is the last installment of the REDEMPTION IN TIME trilogy, a story I have aimed at the reader's forehead, adjusted for range and windage, with a hope to land close to the reader's heart, a good place for any story to end up.

So turn the page, keep your hands and arms inside the car. It's going to be a dark and very dangerous ride. Hopefully I will see you on the other side. Remember: nobody gets off this rock alive...

William Clark/Writer... Michigan/2015...

Chapter One

The waiting was the worst part. The last three seconds before the flash and cold were almost too much. Having gone back twice before, he thought he should be getting used to the mind blowing sensations associated with moving through the Continuum by now. Fat chance!

"Stand by, Commander," announced the voice calmly from outside the phase chamber. "We are going in - 3, 2, 1..."

Seeing the blinding flash and feeling the incredible instantaneous acceleration, he closed his eyes, bit down hard on the mouthpiece, and tucked his chin to chest. He didn't need to see what he was moving through, didn't want to see. Deep heavy sounds of distant thunder vibrated through his body as he picked up speed, the G-force trying to pull him out of the tight fetal position he desperately fought to stay in. *"Hang on, hang on,"* his mind shouted as he fought the rising panic.

All the self doubt, all the emotional reservations about his ability to do this, flooded through his mind. He was not special; he was just a soldier like thousands of others, suddenly finding himself in a position of great expectation and responsibility. He wanted to stop, wanted to not be *that guy*, the one who failed, the human benchmark of what not to be.

In Special Operations, the Operators from JSOC, Dev Group, and DELTA Squadrons, were full of sad examples of guys who made the cut, got selected but failed due to a flaw, a hidden weakness in strength of character. Sometimes it was booze, sometimes women, sometimes a moment of bad judgment that brought it all down, a lifetime of effort and hope reduced to a solitary walk from the commander's office with a form letter in the pocket stating that you were no longer part of something you had lived your whole life to be part of. You had become *"that guy"*.

He was now tumbling, falling at light-speed through the void. He had been told in every briefing prior to the jump that, because of the intense emotional process of going through the Continuum, deep bedrock fears and insecurities could surface to crushing levels. Most came through fine, shaken to the core for only a short time, while others were never the same again and had to be rifted from the program, having come face to face with the reality of who they really were and were not. It was a terrible price to pay for dedication and sacrifice.

He was starting to slow down now, the temperature warming, the flashing lights and sounds becoming less intense. Biting down hard on the mouth guard, he steeled himself for the next sensation - the drop, the landing. Even though he had slowed to a fraction of the phasing speed, the landing was always fast and hard, like stepping out of a moving car going twenty miles an hour. As he slowed down even further, he could feel the temperature drop. *Any second now, hold on, hold on.* A moment later he slammed into the cold snow-covered ground with a thud, tumbling and sliding, finally coming to rest on his back, his heavy gasps sending up small white vapor clouds into the cold night air. "Jesus," he whispered.

After several minutes he sat up, surprised to see that he had landed in what looked like a small park. A light snow was falling, the cool wet flakes landing on his face. As he slowly got to his knees, his vision began to clear. He could see the buildings of the city all around him, the walls painted in the subdued orange glow of streetlights. It was quiet, the falling snow sending a hush through the air. Thirty yards away to his right, a small flatbed truck loaded with barrels slowly puttered along the wet street, its headlights illuminating the steady snowfall.

He got to his feet, brushing the snow off his pants, and checked his gear. The pistol was still secured in a belt holster as was the pouch that held the suppressor and two extra magazines. Suddenly feeling conspicuous standing in the middle of open ground, he started walking towards the street while reaching inside his heavy coat. He could feel the small, garage-door-opener-sized plastic box still hanging around his neck - his ticket home, his lifeline. As he walked, he let the sights, sounds, and smell of the place wash over him. Crossing the street he could hear music faintly playing somewhere in the dark, a piano and laughter drifting through the air. It was comforting, familiar.

As his head cleared, an almost overpowering thirst hit hard, another physical symptom of traveling through the Continuum. The scientists had told him that this would happen, having something to do with the molecular structure of the body being agitated by the jump. Walking past several closed shops, he pulled his collar tight against the cold as he drew closer to the sound of music and raucous laughter. Rounding the corner, he was relieved to see the brightly lit sign of the Sterneckerbrau Tavern. He knew the Hofbra itself was located on the bottom floor of the four-story building. Gilded ornate plaster archways adorned the tavern entrance. It was just like the pictures he had been shown.

The pre-jump briefings and lectures at Langley had been meticulous in detail. Nothing had been left to chance. He had spent weeks memorizing the architecture in the old black and white photos, the street names and addresses of the city. His clothing was handmade, using only material and sewing methods of the time and geographic location. Two weeks prior to the jump he had only eaten the type of food and drink available from the period. Even his haircut and general personal hygiene was studied and modified for the time. He had been amazed that the jump facility prep team even actually had an aerosol spray that when applied gave him the funky body odor appropriate for the period. Correct period currency, along with ironclad identification documents, completed the package. If stopped or questioned by anyone in authority, they would meet a Mister Abel Hauser from Munich, a second-generation pipe fitter with no family, a nobody, just someone who blended with the population, just another face in the grainy black and white crowd.

It was a perception that they counted on; to hide in plain sight was the best of all subterfuge. Stepping through the front door of the expansive bar, he stamped his feet, dropping cold and snow as he quickly surveyed the room. The expansive beer-hall was packed with men drinking, swearing, and singing all at the same time. Unless you were standing six inches away from someone, a normal sound level of conversation was impossible. As he slowly nudged his way through the crowd, he picked up short bits of conversation, the preponderance of dialect carrying a heavy northern Germany color – fast and hard-edged on the consonants, indicative of the Bavarian influence. He understood all of it; his language studies had been spot on. Most of the talk was political in nature, some about work and the drudgery that went with it. Others talked about wives, girlfriends, and the female anatomy in general. Getting to the edge of the crowd he stepped up to the long, black oak bar, motioning to the sweaty bartender. "Ein bier bitte," he announced in perfect German above the din of the room. The bartender nodded that he heard and slid a heavy glass mug of beer in his direction. Sipping the surprisingly cold brew, he checked his pocket watch, noting the time. It was well after eleven at night and the crowd showed no signs of thinning out. In fact, he watched as even more men came through the doors at the far end of the expansive beer hall. He turned back to the bar and caught his own reflection in the large mirror on the wall. It was an odd, disconcerting image that looked back through the haze of pipe and cigarette smoke that now hung heavy in the room, a face, his face of stern determination in a sea of loud, happy drunken men, a face that could give him away as an interloper if he was not careful.

He had been prepped about body language and how he exhibited it. He had to move through the environment with the ease and nonchalance of someone who was born and raised in the time. Things unfamiliar and strange had been addressed and handled as normal and routine. Working to soften the lines in his face, he smiled slightly at himself in the mirror, a false flash of sincerity. He had to project normality when in reality the enormous burden of millions of lives depended on him and the actions he had to take.

He took another sip of his beer and then took several deep breaths, practicing the relaxation techniques he had learned during training. Yoga, biofeedback and visualization were all taught, tools for the toolbox, anything to make him a more proficient killer. He needed to be seen by others in the room. A familiar face was less threatening than a stranger suddenly appearing. He had been sent in two days prior to the day he was supposed to hit his target. He had two days to fit in, two days to be part of this time, this place.

Leaning back against the bar, he quickly raised his mug when a shouted toast roared up from the crowd. "**Genieße das Leben ständig! Du bist länger tot als lebendig!** "He downed the rest of his beer as did the other four hundred plus men in the room and then slammed the heavy mug on the bar. An arousing cheer went up from the crowd as more beer was poured. Turning back to the bar, he ordered another drink and smiled, feeling the soft beer-buzz. The German toast was more than appropriate, translated, "Enjoy the day because you are dead longer than you are alive." Watching the crowd in the mirror, he felt like he was beginning to blend. He was losing his self-consciousness. The smoke, the laughter and the beer pulled him in, wrapping his emotions in a strange softness of peaceful resolve. He would enjoy the day and then in thirty-six hours, sixteen minutes, and 24 seconds, he would blow the brains out of the man he had traveled through space and time to kill. He picked up the second mug and drained half the glass before setting it down. *Yeah, murder most perfect,* he thought. He could drink to that - *definitely.*

Chapter Two

The thick warm trade winds had filled the sails of the Hanna Marie for three days and nights now, pushing the sleek three-masted yacht at a steady ten knots. The skies had been clear, a welcome addition to a, so far, smooth trip from Bora Bora to the kingdom of Tonga. Clark was one of nine passengers that had paid the ten thousand dollars fare that included meals, a comfortable bed in a tiny stateroom, and all the blue water ocean adventure the vast Pacific could provide. He had never been much of a sailor, nor had he spent much time in his life living or visiting the ocean. He was running, knowing full well that powerful forces would eventually track him down; leaving the Island on a small private pleasure yacht would make it harder for those in pursuit.

He needed time to think, time to carefully plan his next move. He climbed the short flight of stairs from his quarters and stepped up on deck, immediately feeling the hot tropical sun and the warm wind wash over his body. "Good morning, Mister Clark", announced one of the crew at the top of the stairs. "Will you be wanting breakfast on deck? I can bring it to you if you'd like."

"Yes, that would be fine. I'll be towards the bow if that's okay?"

The steward smiled. "Very good, sir. I will bring it right up."

Clark nodded and then slowly started making his way along the narrow catwalk towards the front of the yacht. He had been greatly impressed by the service and professionalism of the crew. The ten thousand dollars for the ticket was proving to be money well spent. All he had to do was eat, sleep and get a tan as the yacht, Hanna Marie, out of Barbados slowly made its way on the ten-day journey to Tonga.

Sitting down in one of the small deck chairs, he nodded to the heavily-oiled woman sitting beside him. "Morning."

"Morning," she replied lowering her sunglasses. "How was your rest?"

She was the wife of the German tool and die maker from Hamburg, a middle-aged woman with short blond hair and a rose tattoo on her ankle, who, at an earlier time, had been a real beauty. There were three other couples on the boat, all European. It was a pleasant bunch as travelers go, all sharing the same relaxed way of vacationing most Europeans exhibit. Unlike a lot of American travelers who need to be occupied with some kind of manufactured distraction, his shipmates seemed more than content to sit on the deck, drink their wine, and soak up the tropical sun.

"It was fine," replied Clark smiling. It was amazing how comfortable the Germans were with nudity, he thought. The woman sitting next to him was topless but acted as if nothing was unusual. By the depth of her tan he could see that she was not doing this for effect; this was a lifestyle. *Who was he to say it was wrong*, he thought, smiling.

"Here is you breakfast, sir," announced the steward, stepping up while lowering a tray of coffee, mixed fruits, and rolls. "Let me know if there is anything else you need."

Clark set the tray on his lap. "No. I'm good. Thank you."

A sudden heavy swell splashed a wake against the hull sending a fine mist over the bow. "Ahh....that's nice," announced the woman adjusting herself in the chair, the water droplets looking like diamonds on her dark skin.
Clark squinted as he looked up into the midmorning sun. "It really is beautiful out here," he replied sipping his coffee. "I

could get used to this."

"Is this your first time on one of these trips, Mister Clark?"

"Yes. By the way, you can call me Dave." He reached over and shook hands with the woman.

"I'm Zoe, Dave. My pleasure." Her hand was slick with warm oil.

"Good morning."

Clark looked up and saw the woman's husband walking over. "Good morning."

He shook hands and then took a chair on the other side of his wife. "Beautiful day, huh?" he announced smiling. To Clark, the man looked to be in his early sixties and was wearing one of those typical European Speedos that any self-respecting male over the age of fifteen would never wear. Looking at a senior citizen with a large beer belly wearing that thing was something you just did not need to see before ten o'clock in the morning.

"So, you are an American?" questioned the German as he adjusted his chair. For the rest of the morning the three sat and talked and drank until lunch. During that time Clark learned his traveling companions took this trip every year, they had two grown sons in college, and they were seriously thinking about retiring in Bora Bora. As for Clark, he kept the details about his life to a minimum, telling them that he was a divorced schoolteacher from Boise, Idaho, all lies, of course. Telling them the truth, that he was an FBI agent on the run from his own organization and that he was wanted by a shadowy group of government shot-callers who had just launched a drone strike on the Vatican, might be a little much. The only reason he was on the boat in the first place was to buy some time. If the truth were told, the ocean scared the shit out of him. So far the only real redeeming value on the whole trip was Zoe's big, round, oiled up tits.

Aside from all that, he let himself relax, allowing the early afternoon sun to sizzle away on his skin. Three beers and a Club sandwich later he was well on his way to a pretty terrific afternoon on the deep end of the blue Pacific.

As the day wore on, a small, growing sense of dread took seed in his mind. Maybe the booze was wearing off or maybe the sledgehammer weight of the reality of his true situation was becoming clear. He had escaped the Vatican attack by pure chance. Because one of his captors had a guilty conscience, he had been set free with a bag of money, a set of strange medallions, a well-worn diary of a past fugitive, and a one-way ticket to anywhere. On the surface it would sound like a pretty good deal, but a hundred grand and nowhere safe to go darkened the picture quite a bit. Thinking back to the Robashaw diary, he could see now why the old man had stayed on the run so long

Clark had lost everything but his life, leaving him with no family, no career, no friends to turn to, only a couple hundred thousand dollars in cash, the medals, and the clothes on his back. He sipped the last of the last beer he was going to drink that night as he watched the German couple slowly dance on the deck. It was now early evening, and he was talked out. He was starting to feel a headache take root behind his left eye. It always did that when he drank too much, his body's way of shutting down the urge, closing the desire. Feeling a strong piss coming on, he bid his German friends good night and slowly made his way off the Bow deck and back to his cabin. On his way down the stairs below deck, one of the stewards asked him if he wanted supper on deck. "No, thanks. I'm just going to go to bed early," he replied. He really was tired, and a good night's sleep just might be what he needed.

Before drifting off a short while later, his thoughts briefly ran the gamut of blind fear of what the future might hold to the soft, lower belly tingle image of Zoe's big oiled up boobs. There were worst things to fall asleep thinking about.... far worse.

***

Donald Pell Junior liked his job, enjoyed the power the position brought. The pay was decent; GS 13 by age 36 wasn't bad. Good family with old money and connections, top grades at Auburn, graduate studies at George Town, and a three-year stint with the First Ranger Battalion as a First Lieutenant rounded out the picture of a guy who had hit all the shiny spots in the Government matrix for success. He had the looks and the pedigree for all the good stuff the heavy hitters had to offer.

Don Senior had been a minor cabinet appointee during the Clinton years, running an obscure yet influential organization that controlled foreign aid to Third World countries – USACORP. Its public mantra was American rice, beans, and barley for the starving wretches. It's true stock and trade was bullets, guns, and dark-side training for anyone who wanted to help further the cause of whoever was in power at the White House at the time.

All the three letter agencies had funneled people and hardware through the USACORP pipeline for years. Whenever some up-and-comer needed his ticket punched, he was sent to some Third World shit hole to get a few good kills to gain the rep needed to be a part of the club. The cycle went on well after the womanizing hillbilly left the White House, lasting far into the Bush forty-one years. After 9-11 it was easy to get people who needed an "outside the wire" field trip where all the right people got smoked and the good guys went back to Crystal City on expanse accounts and two martini lunches. It bought membership in the clique, where all the cool guys are in on the joke, leaving the general public in the dark and the bush shitter down range catching the heat.

His dedication to the cause had not disappointed his handlers at the Kingdom, the intelligence insiders' name for the stand-alone organization that drew talent from all the three letter agencies in the shadow world. Pell's mandate from higher was to find Agent Clark and kill him with no revocation, no vagaries in the order, nothing that could be misread or misconstrued. This was a direct-line elimination order that was to be carried out as quickly as possible. FBI Agent David Clark, credential number 17925, had been deemed, labeled, and charged as an enemy of the United States Government and that was it.

Pell was standing on the small dock watching the sunset when his cell phone rang. "Yes, sir."

"Don, this is Pryor. How close are you to the package?"

Pell recognized the voice of Mike Pryor, the Deputy Operations Chief of Staff at the Kingdom, a no-nonsense ex-Marine gunny who sported a consummate crew cut and a face right out of central casting of movie thugs from the thirties.

"The package is on a charted yacht; left Bora Bora three days ago," he replied, nudging a small pile of blue green seagull shit over the edge of the dock.

"You have a fix on where it's headed?" questioned Pryor.

"Yes, sir. Tonga. I will be catching my flight in the morning. I'll be there several days before the yacht gets to port."

"I don't think I need to tell you how clean this needs to be, do

I, Don?"

Pell smiled. "No sir, I understand how important this is."

There was a pause on the phone. Pell wasn't sure if Pryor was keeping a dramatic pause for effect or if he just needed to think of what to say next.

"All right, Don. Keep me posted and get this done."

Pell nodded as he watched an elderly Asian couple walk by, folks taking an evening walk in the warm trade wind breeze. "Yes, sir. I'm on it." Before Pell could say goodbye, Pryor ended the call from his end, having said what he needed to say.

Pell downed the last of his beer while watching the setting sun turn into a fiery red ball on the horizon. He had arrived in Bora Bora three days behind Clark and soon learned that the agent had bought himself some time by taking a slow boat to nowhere. No, this would be coming to a close pretty quick in Pell's mind. He would get to Tonga tomorrow, wait for Clark to show, and clip him before he knew what hit him. He set his empty Corona bottle on the dock railing and started walking back to the hotel. In a few days he would kill Agent Clark, doing his duty to God and Country and then move on to the next operation. He smiled to himself at the thought that he was actually getting paid for this kind of work.

Yeah, tomorrow he would put his game-face on, but tonight he was going to have himself a diversion with the pretty French dining room waitress at the hotel. She had agreed to drinks after her shift, good looking, not too bright, and spoke limited English. Best of all, she had a thing for Americans... perfect. *Yeah, life was good* he thought walking through the cool air-conditioned lobby to the restaurant. *Not bad at all.*

Chapter Three

Hauser stretched and then rubbed the sleep out of his eyes. He had been dozing since dawn, but now the heavy traffic noise outside the boarding house had made sound sleep impossible. Throwing back the thick wool blankets, he sat up immediately feeling the chill in the small room. Dark wood paneling covered the walls. A small sink stood in the corner. He shared a bathroom down the hall with the loud talking and heavy smoking lodgers occupying the floor's four other rooms.

He had slept as if in a coma, a deep and dreamless sleep like he had never experienced before. This along with a litany of other symptoms had been described to him by the doctors and scientists in preparation for making the jump. Now sitting on the side of the bed as he pulled on his clothes, he began to make note of the sore throat and the odd copper taste, like he had been sucking on a mouthful of pennies. The doctors had explained that this strange but not debilitating side effect would be due to the blood's elevated PH levels after traveling through the Continuum.

Running his hands under the ice-cold tap water, he shivered more from excitement than the chill in the room. Here he was - 1939 prewar Germany. He had been given a tremendous opportunity, a mission that was far beyond anything his imagination could have conceived.

All men want to have their lives mean something, to have it count, to be validated. Most go through life waiting for that chance, a chance that never presents itself. They live a life of half-truth, one of partial victories and heavy compromises. Most live a reactive existence, dancing to the music of others. For most men, moments of true clarity are rare. They come unexpectedly, sometimes from fear, some in sorrow, and some through trauma. But for most, clarity comes when the heart is at rest and the mind is open no matter what the cause.

He looked into the cracked mirror above the sink, remembering one of his moments. It was back at BUDS training in Coronado, sixty years from now. It was the fifth day of Hell Week, and the eighty-seven candidates of his class had already been whittled down to half that number. They had been doing a night beach run when their instructors commanded that they stop, sit with arms locked together in the fifty-eight degree water, and wait until they were given the command to get up and resume the run. He smiled slightly at his image, remembering how bone chilling cold the ocean had been that night. He had never been more miserable. The instructors had had a large fire on the beach, a tantalizing yet cruel thing to see thirty yards away as he sat in freezing water shivering uncontrollably. He thought back to the moment when the instructor had stepped up to the water's edge and matter-of-factly announced that if anyone wanted to quit and warm themselves by the fire, now would be the time to do it. Having had enough, several of the men had stood and walked out of the water over the next hour. They had reached their moment of clarity, a painful truth in their lives. They did not have the mental strength to continue. They would never wear the Trident. As those few had stood by the fire, already regretting their choices, he had remained in the dark and freezing water coming to his own moment of clarity; he would die before he would quit. Here he would make his stand. There would be no going back. It was at that moment that he surrendered to something bigger than himself. He let it all go at the speed of thought and crossed the threshold from good to greatness in strength. A hundred and seventy-eight meateaters started his class, all wanting the privilege of becoming a SEAL. Nineteen graduated. He had been one of them.

It was that resolve, that dedication to the cause that had brought him into this program. He was now a government 'viable' asset, a tool to be used. He had no illusions about how his handlers *really* felt about him. He had a skill-set and the guts to use it, and that was it. If he failed or faltered, he would be discarded. The United States Intelligence Community had a very short memory when it came to its heroes. The reputation that they sacrificed their own on a regular basis was well deserved.

He checked himself in the mirror one last time while pulling on his coat. In less than twenty hours he would have a chance to prove himself and end a horror before it could start. "You got this," he whispered to his image before turning to leave.

As he left the room he could smell brewing coffee mingled with the odor of stale cigarette smoke. As he had rented his room the night before he had been hit with the realization that in 1939 every adult he had come across smoked and that every building reeked from the harsh German tobacco.

As he stepped out of the hotel and into the cold morning sunshine, he wondered how many of the people he saw walking on the sidewalks would soon be dead, how many of these "good" Germans would have been directly killed in the madness that was about to be unleashed?

Pulling his collar tight, he quickly headed across the wide busy street towards the Voltsenhub Café on the corner, a small midtown bistro that served the shopkeepers and working class up-and-comers that populated this part of the city. He would get a hard roll and sausage along with a heavy mug of strong coffee. He would read the Munich newspaper, *Vossische Zeitung,* knowing that it would be filled with editorials and opinions, a virtual frenzy of information concerning the past exploits of his target and his approaching arrival. It was like the whole country was in the process of a collective nervous breakdown, blind to the cause, like a mother screaming a lullaby, an insanity with purpose.

The cancer had been spreading since that unseasonably cold November day in 1923. The "Beer Hall Putch", as it was later called, had been a bloody two-day political revolt that began with a young, fire-in-the-eye Hitler and six hundred of his rabid followers occupying the Munich beer hall *Burgerbraukeller.* Adolf Hitler, a decorated World War One soldier had become a rising star in the NSDAP, the raw, sharp-edged beginnings of the Nazi party. The bloodshed had started with the young Hitler firing a pistol shot through the ceiling of the crowded hall and announcing that he and his NSDAP thugs were now in charge of the German Government. For two days bloody street battles had ensued, ending with four German police officers and sixteen Nazis dead. Countless had been injured and Hitler, the spark that had lit the flame of unrest, had been arrested, tried, and sentenced to five years in prison for treason.

Now, sixteen years later, Hitler was the Fuhrer of Germany, the sole totalitarian leader of the government. On the eve of his order to invade Poland, he would be giving a speech in the same Munich Beer Hall where it all started. Among the delirious cheering crowd, Hauser would be waiting, a single human island of sanity in an ocean of near hysteria. He would take his time, move with the crush of the crowd, and at the opportune moment, fire a suppressed forty-caliber slug through Hitler's skull. The beast would be dead before he hit the floor. With this one act, he would save millions of lives and the horror of mass slaughter would be stopped before it started. History would change at the speed of a bullet. His window of opportunity to make the shot would be miniscule, a second, maybe two. In the ensuing chaos, his escape timeline would be cut even closer. It would be a grand endeavor by anyone's definition.

He knew that Hitler was rarely otherwise within reach of a pistol shot as he moved from location to location. The SS guards, both uniformed and the plainclothes who blended with the crowd, seemed to have a sixth sense about the Fuehrer's protection. He had studied the archived films, watched the way that Hitler moved through massive crowds of prewar Germany. It seemed that there was always an overly large corridor he moved through, either by vehicle or on foot. This had been done for several reasons. First, Hitler's movements were filmed as a propaganda tool. The images of wide cathedral-like vistas of a single warrior taking on the mantel of ethereal leadership from the Germanic gods set his leadership apart from the masses. Secondly, it had been done for protection. In all the perceived physical interaction with the German people, Hitler had never been seen actually touching any of his hysterical followers. He had instead been filmed with a small number of close confidants at his home or in meticulously planned events strictly with military officers and underlings. It was well known within his inner circle that the Fuhrer hated being touched, finding physical interaction repulsive and avoiding it whenever possible. It was a quirk of personality that suited the level of protection the lethal SS bodyguards wanted for their leader.

The meeting in the Munich beer hall was the break in protection protocol that would be exploited as the auditorium's six hundred capacity was considered a small gathering by Nazi standards. It would be by invitation only. Through exhaustive research from scientists and government archivists of this time, a replica of the Nazi party's hand-signed invitations for the event had been created for Abel Hauser, a lowly pipefitter from Munich. If all things went according to plan, World War Two would be stopped before it started… an honorable endeavor, indeed.

Chapter Four

The hot Pacific sun was just beginning to set on the far horizon as the Hanna Marie slowly, quietly eased up to the dock in the sleepy port of Nukualofa Tonga, eight days after leaving Bora Bora. As he climbed down onto the pier, Clark could hear music thumping down from one of the beach's open-air bars. It had been a full, nine-day voyage, and his gait and balance were a bit unsteady as he retrieved his bag. He headed up the dock after giving his word to the Captain that he would check in with passport control in the morning, something he had no intention of doing.

Finally, standing on dry ground, he could see that the beachfront bar was jammed with sweaty tourists all dancing badly to the reggae beat from the out-of-tune Rastafarian trio playing on the small stage. Even though the sun was now a purple and orange spray of light far out on the ocean, it was still at least ninety degrees outside. Rivulets of sweat ran down his back as he made his way up to the taxi stand near the street.

He liked the tropics, liked the way his body felt from the heat. It eased his joints and loosened the tension in his back that he always felt in the colder climates of the States. Somehow the tropics always felt like home. It was this ease of spirit that he needed to be most aware of, the false sense that he was okay and just another European on vacation, intent on finding the things that do not really exist in exotic places.

Every exotic location is home to people who do not think of it as anything other than home, for the locals of the "Exotics" raise kids, pay bills, and go to work just like the schoolteacher in Ohio or the taxi cab driver in West Sussex. A stranger to the soft rhythm of the tropics could get lost in the warm night breeze. The thick smell of saltwater and wild jasmine could bend the head for days or even years if not checked. Staying *in check* was something Clark intended to do. He would stay focused, he thought, as he settled into the back seat of the cab.

The sweaty black driver turned around. "Where to, boss?" he asked smiling, a silver tooth catching the light. The car smelled of stale beer and cardboard strawberry air fresheners, the cheap kind that you buy in gas stations that look like small pine trees or cherries.

Clark thought for a moment as several more half-drunk British tourists walked noisily by. The party in the beach bar was breaking up, the revelers trying to hail cabs while puking and pissing on the sidewalk. It was just another night in paradise. "Take me to the White Sands Beach resort."

The driver turned back to the wheel and dropped the crank on the meter. "Okay, Boss."

Clark sat back and let the night breeze coming in through the window take him back to the time when he and his wife Donna had spent a week at the White Sands, a lifetime ago. She still loved him then, would hold his hand when they walked, and give herself willingly in the dark. It was a time in their lives when they could communicate without saying a word, both hearing the same white noise of caring and commitment that happily married couples could hear. It had been wonderful.

As they drove through the dark streets, his mind was on better days, carefree blocks of time when the only worries were small... did he buy enough travelers checks for the vacation or what was he going to have for dinner at the hotel. He smiled to himself remembering how excited Donna had been when they first arrived on the island, how she fought sleep because she did not want to waste a minute of time even though she was exhausted from the nineteen-hour flight. She had fallen asleep on their room's small balcony on their first night in Tonga, and he had picked her up like a sleeping child and put her to bed later that night. He had drifted off listening to her deep breathing and the small waves breaking on the beach. He had never been happier.

As if startled from a deep sleep, he snapped out of the nostalgic fog, focusing back to the drive through the dark countryside on their way out to the White Sands Hotel. The air rushing in from the window was cooler now and carried the comforting familiar scent of salt water. They were getting close. Even though he had slept and lounged on the yacht during the trip over, he was tired and was looking forward to a comfortable bed that wasn't moving with the rhythm of the ocean.

Maybe it was the heat, maybe he was far more tired then he thought, but he never saw the car a quarter mile behind. If he had watched closely, he would have sensed that it was following them. "How much farther?" he asked, looking at the driver's eyes in the rearview mirror.

"Not far. It's just up the road," replied the man smiling. "It's a very nice place."

Clark nodded. "Yes it is." The driver began to slow the car and then made a left onto a gravel drive that meandered through the tall trees and bushy undergrowth. The headlights caught the green-eyed reflections of small Gecko lizards as the head lights swept across the bush. Two long lazy turns later and the brightly lit front entrance of the White Sands Hotel came into view. He smiled seeing the lights. Nothing had changed. The place looked just as it had when he and Donna had first seen the place years ago.
Blinded by the memories of his past, he got out of the cab, again failing to notice the small sedan that had eased into the far side of the resort parking lot and turned off its lights.

"How much do I owe you?" questioned Clark leaning into the passenger side window of the cab. It felt good to get into the fresh air and away from the overpowering smell of strawberry air freshener.

"Ah, twenty-one fifty."

"You take American currency? That's all I have."

The cabbie smiled. "Everyone takes American cash, boss. No problem."

Clark handed the driver thirty dollars. "Keep the change."

"You sure, Boss? You might need to buy some good Tonga beer later," replied the driver smiling.

Clark slung his knapsack over his shoulder. "No, it's fine. Thanks again. Have a good night."

The cabbie smiled and then dropped the car in gear. "Thanks, boss. Listen. If you need anything while you're here…. here is my card. I know a lot of cool places and many beautiful Tonga women, very clean. I can fix you up."

Clark stepped back from the car and laughed. "Naw, that's okay. I just need to get some sleep. But thanks anyway." The cabbie gave him a thumbs-up and then slowly drove away laughing. As tempting as it might have been to have some female company, Clark knew that he was not on vacation. His situation was tenuous at best, and any local entanglements or distractions would only complicate matters more. Travel light, travel fast, and most of all, travel quiet.
Instinctively he knew that bad things were not too far behind. It was only a matter of days, maybe hours, before they tracked him down. The Kingdom had worldwide reach and would not rest until he had been dealt with.

Walking towards the brightly lit lobby to check in, he decided that he wasn't hungry enough to postpone sleep. He would try to get a good eight hours of uninterrupted rest and then make plans to get off the island as quietly as possible. Just as he reached the large double glass doors of the hotel lobby, hurried footsteps crunching on the gravel driveway could be heard coming fast.

"Mister Clark, I need to talk to you," announced the man walking up.

For a fleeting second Clark thought about ignoring the voice as a chill ran up his sweat-soaked back. They had found him. He pushed his way through the heavy doors and faced the man who was now right behind him. If this was to be his assassination, it would have to be done in front of the desk clerk.

Clark had never seen the man before. He was tall with light brown hair cut short with the build of an athlete. Clark guessed his age to be about thirty.

"Who are you?" Clark asked stepping into the center of the lobby.

The man stepped up close, a humorless grin curled up on the left side of his face. "My name is Pell. I've been waiting for you."

"Yeah, what for?"

Pell nodded. "Listen, pard, you can make this easy or hard, but we need to step outside."

Clark smiled. "You been practicing that line, Pell? I have no idea who you are or what you want, so you do whatever you think you need to do. I am going to check in and then go to sleep. So fuck off!"

Pell leaned up close. "Listen, asshole. You got about a second to start moving towards the door before things get compl...."
Clark cut him off with a vicious upper cut punch, snapping Pell's head back as if he had been shot. He never saw it coming and dropped to the floor in a heap, the back of his head striking the white marble floor with a thud. The startled desk clerk stood open-mouthed behind the counter, stunned by what he had just seen.

"It's okay. It's all right," Clark announced loudly to the bewildered clerk. "This is my brother in law. He's had too much to drink. I'll take care of him." He bent over the unconscious assassin and quickly dragged him out of the lobby onto the gravel driveway. He did a quick frisk and found the suppressed Beretta 9 mm in the back of Pell's waistband. *The arrogance of this prick*, thought Clark, *he must have really thought he could just walk up and intimidate me into going with him.* Pell was just starting to come around as Clark dragged him further into the shadows. Not wanting him to get on his feet just yet, Clark stood up and kicked Pell as hard as he could in the groin. The stunning blow rolled him into a tight fetal position with a half-conscious moan.

Clark then went through his pockets and found his car keys and wallet.

"Is everything all right?" asked the still bewildered desk clerk, now standing just outside the doors.
Clark stepped out of the shadows smiling. "Oh yeah. He's all right. He's just throwing up from too much rum. I'll get him back to his hotel."

The clerk thought for moment. "I have a brother in law that acts just like that."

"Yeah, but you know family," replied Clark laughing, relieved that the clerk was buying the story. He looked back in the dark and saw that Pell was slowly rolling over onto his side. "Well, sorry for the trouble. I'd better get him back to my sister. She'll be worried," announced Clark as calmly as he could.

Still not sure of what was going on, but not really wanting to get involved in a family fight, the clerk waved and then slowly walked back through the lobby doors, disappearing inside. Pell was now on his hands and knees, struggling to stand up. Seeing that the clerk was safely inside, Clark quickly trotted over and kicked Pell as hard as he could in the face, knocking him out cold.

Within minutes he found Pell's rental car at the far end of the parking lot, threw his backpack in the back seat, and stuffed Pell's unconscious body in the trunk. Ten minutes later, as he drove, trying to think about his next move, he could hear Pell groaning. Hating the thought but at the same time knowing it was what he had to do, he pulled off the main road onto the first dirt lane he saw. He needed answers and quick. Dark and powerful forces were closing fast, and his life expectancy was now measured in hours, maybe minutes.

After driving farther down the deserted road, he slowly pulled over, turned off his lights, rolled his window down and sat in the dark, listening. No dogs were barking nor were any house lights visible. This was as good a place as any.

Pell was now loudly thumping around in the trunk, apparently recovered from his beating. Before getting out of the car, Clark checked the Beretta. The magazine was full and the suppressor was correctly attached. Under the glow of the dome light he could see that the weapon had no serial numbers. The suppressor was high quality, right out of Government stock. *It was the firearm of a pro, someone experienced at killing close up, a weapon in stark contrast to the idiot in the trunk*, he thought, stepping out of the car. *A trained assassin would never have shown his face, never would have placed himself in front of possible witnesses in the same location as the hit. Pell was either incredibly arrogant or incredibly stupid*, he thought, opening the trunk.

In the dim glow of the trunk light, Clark could see that Pell had been bleeding profusely from the kick in the face. "You broke my nose you, son of a bitch," he hissed wiping his blood-smeared arm across his face.

Clark cocked the hammer on the pistol and pressed the barrel hard into Pell's thigh. "Listen carefully. I am going to ask you questions, and you're going to answer. If you give me any more problems, I am going to shoot you with your own gun in all of your joints, and then I am going to lock you back in this trunk where you will die. Understand?"

"Kiss my ass, you son of a..." *Phat.* The suppressed pistol jumped in Clark's hand, sending a hundred and fifteen grain subsonic bullet smashing through Pell's femur and out the back of his thigh. Pell screamed in agony while gripping his upper leg with both hands.

Clark reached in and roughly covered the man's mouth with his hand. "Shut the hell up. Take the pain, tough guy. You keep screaming, I'll put another one through your eye. Understand? Look at me, Pell. Do you understand?"
Pell nodded, his eyes wide with rage and pain. "Okay," he grunted. "Ask your questions."

Clark reached down and roughly pulled Pell out of the trunk, dropping him on the ground behind the car. "All right, what agency are you from? Who sent you after me?"

"Jesus, I'm bleeding out here," gasped Pell. "Get me to a

doctor."

Clark knelt down and tapped the barrel hard on top of Pell's head. "Listen, dip-shit, the only reason you're still alive is that you have information I need. You don't want to talk – it ends right now." He cocked the hammer on the Beretta and pressed the barrel to Pell's forehead. "Your call. You got three seconds, one, two..."

"Okay, all right," replied Pell in agony. "Goddamn, you have no idea how bad this hurts?"

Clark de-cocked the pistol. "Let's try this again, pal. Who sent you and what were your orders?"

"DIA, I work for the DIA on loan to the Kingdom. My orders were to track you down and kill you."

'That simple, huh?"

"Yeah, that simple, asshole."
"Then why didn't you do it? What was that bullshit at the hotel? What kind of half-ass killer are you anyway?"

Pell groaned. The blood oozing through his fingers looked black in the moonlight. "I didn't think you would be much of a problem. Shit..... I'm gonna puke. You gotta get me to a doc."
Clark stood up and moved a step away as Pell wretched. "Jesus, I'm dying," whispered Pell, falling back in the wet grass. "I'm begging you. Please, get me to a hospital... please."

Standing there in the dark, hearing the breeze blow through the palm trees, Clark was suddenly struck by how surreal it all felt. The man writhing in pain at his feet was dying by inches, suffering in agony from a wound he had caused, yet the detachment he felt from the current reality could not be stronger. The intensity of the moment had pulled him out of who he was like an invisible scalpel, splitting him in two, allowing the spirit to rise into the warm tropical air. He was an observer, watching it all from a strangely detached perspective. Causing Pell more pain or relieving his agony held equal value in Clark's mind. At that moment it really made no difference. He had crossed an emotional bridge he never knew existed.

Curious to see how it would feel and because he instinctively knew Pell was dying, he raised the pistol and fired. *Phat , phat, phat.* The three rounds crashed into the side of Pell's face, blowing out large pieces of skull and jaw. This was just a macabre formality. He had killed the man the moment he had shot him in the leg. It was an emotional bridge indeed.

Chapter Five

Hammond Shaw had been in the Phasing Lab since five that morning. He had skipped breakfast, missed lunch, and now noticed the reflection of the mercury vapor streetlights in the expansive parking lot four stories below. Fighting a losing battle with a growing headache, he sat down behind his desk at the far end of the lab and glanced at the time on the large wall clock. It was seven fifteen. He had worked fourteen hours straight without a break. The day crew, men and women with real lives that flourished far beyond the highly classified confines of the lab, had long since left.

As the lead scientist, he was expected to put in these kinds of hours. He had been entrusted with the responsibility of overseeing the greatest scientific endeavor since the NASA moon-landing project, a responsibility that had become his life. Theory had become reality for the scientific community on his watch. Two years earlier, not too far from where the current facility stood, Dr. Taylor, an aeronautical engineer and physicist working out of the Sandi National Labs in New Mexico, had become the first to unravel the staggering complexity of time travel.

Working out of his basement, he had perfected the use of the Casmir Vacuum in stabilization of both ends of a projected wormhole allowing time dilation. By channeling massive amounts of electrical power through conducting plates and non-linear crystals, he had been able to produce usable Dark Matter as a secondary propellant. It had been a staggering feat considering he had been working alone and with limited resources. Prior to his discovery only miniscule amounts of Dark Matter had ever been created. The Hedron Collider had accomplished this in 2011, becoming the first particle accelerator in the world to do so.

"So, how is our boy doing?" questioned Dr. Reese, sitting

down at the large array console. Reese was one of the lead scientists working on the project and Shaw's go-to source for information regarding quantum gravity and orbital inclination. A man in his late sixties, he carried the classic look of the befuddled physics professor - a man thirty pounds overweight with disheveled hair and perpetually dirty glasses. He had a body odor that ranged from mildly offensive to full-blown biohazard noxious. In fact, it was bad enough at times for Shaw to mention it. On those occasions a look of embarrassed befuddlement would cross the older man's face and he would soon reappear with matted damp hair dressed in the same clothes he had been wearing earlier.

Aside from his dubious lack of attention to hygiene, he was a genuinely upbeat congenial person to be around. All of his personal foibles had long since been excused due to his towering intellect and his uncanny ability to break down mind-numbingly complicated quantum mathematics into understandable sets of applicable equations. To Shaw, who had personally recruited him from Bell Laboratories several years earlier, he was the smartest man he had ever known.

Shaw checked the biorhythm readings on the computer. "Looks like he is awake and moving; all indicators are solid and holding," he replied as he sipped his now cold coffee. "What are you doing here so early? I thought you didn't come in till seven thirty or so?"

"Ah, you know me. I can't stand the idea of not being here while the jump is in progress. Too afraid I'm going to miss something," replied Reese sitting back in his chair smiling.

Shaw nodded as he adjusted one of the Spatial Coordinate indicators. "Yep. I know what you mean. This really is an incredible event. The idea of missing any of it for sleep is unbearable."
Reese scribbled several more calculations into his notebook. "I've made some notes concerning some of the social impact

considerations. Would you be interested in hearing them?" he asked, looking up, adjusting his glasses.

"Are your notes going to ruin my perfect evening?" Shaw asked, sitting back in his chair.

He knew that no matter what he said, Reese would tell him what was on his mind, either verbally or in stacks of paper notes to be left on his desk. "I would be delighted to hear what you have come up with, my friend. I learn something more from you every time we talk."

Missing the mild sarcasm, Reese cleared his throat and straightened his notes. "Are you aware of how many people died as a direct result of World War Two?"

Shaw shook his head. "I'm not sure, but I would guess that the number would be in the millions."

Reese looked up from his notes. "Over seventy-two million," he announced quietly. "I've checked my calculations against all known records of listed casualties, and seventy-two million is very close."

"What are you getting at?" questioned Shaw, already knowing the answer.

"Well, I know you and I have had this discussion before, but I have not stopped thinking about the possible, I dare say catastrophic, consequences of our endeavor here."

Shaw closed his notepad. "Harold, you do understand that we are just the facilitators on this project. The possible ramifications of what is going on with this program have been discussed and a plan of action agreed upon, a plan way above our pay grade."

Reese adjusted his glasses and looked back at his notes, his level of agitation starting to rise. "Yes, I am well aware of the fact that others are making these final decisions. But how can we be sure the *right* decisions are being made?" He rolled his chair closer, holding out his stack of notes. "Do these decision makers actually realize that the microsecond our assassin puts a bullet through the brain of Adolf Hitler in the year of 1939 seventy-two million people who died as a direct result of the conflict will instantly be alive. In addition to that, the number of people who were *directly* involved, family members, etc, will make that well over two hundred million. That is not even counting the number who died years later from wounds. I just think we are collectively naïve."

Shaw thought for a moment. "Harold, are you losing faith in the project? A lack of resolve can be dangerous in this environment."

"No, Hammond, I am not losing faith in our ability to make this work," replied Reese lowering his voice. "I am questioning the idea that it's the right thing to do to begin with. Just because you have the ability to do something doesn't necessarily mean you should do it. My God, our actions could conceivably end existence as we know it. Are we *really* willing to take that risk? The Rubinstein theory of parallel dimensional shift and chronology patterns is just that - a theory. It is hardly enough to build a program around."

Shaw eased back in his chair and laid his glasses on the counsel counter. He had thought in depth about the consequences and possible ramifications of what could happen if Hitler died before the war. He also had thought about the staggering amount of human suffering and pain that would be negated if the mad man could be killed before major hostilities began. Six million Jews would be spared. Another twenty million Soviets would survive, not having been fed into the meat grinder of the Eastern front. Countless lives would be saved...countless. In his mind, it was a risk worth taking.

"Harold, I believe in this. World War Two was terrible...beyond terrible.... and all caused by one man. If we have the ability to erase that stain, that cancer, then I am all for it. I honestly think this is for the greater good. I really do."

Reese shook his head. "What do you think God thinks about this?"

"I didn't think you were a religious man, Harold. As far as God is concerned, I think he checked out of the equation the minute the SS started pouring Zyclon B gas pellets down those air vents. That's where I think God fits in all of this."

Reese sat back in his chair in deep thought. "You know, Hammond, if I really thought you felt that way, I'm not sure I would have taken this position. Surely you don't discount the possible spiritual ramifications of what we are doing here?"

"I am very much aware of the possible, if not probable, consequences of this project, Harold, but in the heart of logic, as I see it, the cost is worth the final result. If I did not believe that, I would have not taken the job." He leaned forward in his chair. "Are your trepidations going to interfere with what has to be done here?" he asked softly.

Reese thought for a moment. "No," he replied with a sigh. "This is the greatest discovery in the history of Mankind. As a scientist, I would be a fool to walk away from it. I just wanted to express my thoughts as both a scientist and as someone with a spiritual concern."
Shaw smiled. "Your concerns are noted, my friend, and are probably well founded to some extent. Thank you for sharing them with me. Did you say you have notes and data on your findings?"

"Yes, several notebooks full. I have been collecting them in a locked cabinet in my workspace. Is there a problem?"

Shaw shook his head. "No, no problem. I just need to be sure that none of the information, notes, etc, ever leaves the office. This work, as you know, is beyond classified."

Reese looked generally surprised that Shaw would even bring up the obvious classified level of the project. "Yes, of course," he replied softly. A strange feeling of dread suddenly washed over him as he straightened his notes. It was a feeling that he had just crossed a very dangerous boundary.

Shaw smiled and handed him several computer printouts. "Okay then, here are the latest bio sensor readings from the last scan. Look them over if you would. I need to check the oscillation parameters." He patted Reese on the shoulder as he walked by, heartbroken at the chain of events that had just now been set in motion.

Within the realm of scientific measurement, there were levels of tolerance that could only be calculated with an electron microscope, spaces as thin as a human cell and smaller. Within the security protocols of Stone Gate, the level of tolerance for dissent was even less.

The small micro receiver Shaw wore under his lab coat lapel had recorded every bit of his conversation with Reese, transmitting that conversation in real time to a human operator in a third floor office directly below the lab. One of the more distasteful aspects of Shaw's Director responsibilities was the need to monitor all of his project subordinates. All "nonbelievers" were discovered and dealt with by the Kingdom, no matter how much of a role they had played with Stone Gate. The project had been deemed that important. Reese had written his own death warrant the moment he started writing down his insecurities about the program.

The next morning on page 3A of the Washington Post, a small paragraph and grainy black and white photo of Harold Reese would be listed. The single paragraph for the story would read.

Long time Bell Laboratory researcher, Dr. Harold Reese, was found dead in his Crystal City apartment early this morning, the victim of an apparent heart attack. The sixty-six year old Reese lived alone, having relocated to Washington last year. He worked part time as a government consultant.

Shaw slowly poured himself a cup of coffee in the break room before heading across the lab to the dynamic oscillation monitors. He needed a moment to steady himself, to mentally absorb the terrible things that were about to happen. He had known Harold twenty years and the last thing he needed now was for anyone else in the lab to see the stress tremor in his hands or the weakness in his knees as he walked by. *Jesus, the price for all this was high,* he thought sipping his coffee, fighting back the tears...*Maybe too high.*

Chapter Six

Hauser stood on the curb with his collar up and hands buried deep in his pockets as the surprisingly heavy truck and car traffic rumbled by. He had been walking the streets most of the early morning, getting a feel of the city. This was a once in a lifetime trip, and he wanted to soak up as much of the experience as he could with the limited amount of time he had left. The large clock above the bakery on the other side of the wide street struck a bell tone, its chime easily heard above the din of traffic noise. He checked his pocket watch and smiled at how close both timepieces were... five-thirty on the nose.

The rally was scheduled to start at seven, which gave him ample time to get to the hall and find a decent position where he could make the shot. As he walked, a cold gusty wind was at his back carrying the smell of truck exhaust and wet streets. A light cold sprinkle, just above snow, had started to fall as he quickly walked by brightly lit restaurant and storefront windows. Several times he caught his reflection in the glass. A man hunched to the cold in a Stroker cap, baggy pants, and a dark blue wool coat looked back at him. He was amazed at how well he blended in with the rest of the pedestrian traffic. Except for the occasional woman's scarf in bright orange red or blue they all seemed to be wearing the same drab color palette in clothing. He looked like one of them, just another slightly disheveled working class laborer walking the streets of Munich.

He pulled from his coat pocket a fist-sized hard roll that he had bought at the café that morning and began to eat it as he walked. He liked the anonymity, the hiding-in-plain-sight kind of feeling he had as he moved through the people on the sidewalk. He was now confident enough in his appearance and demeanor to nod and smile at several of the locals who walked by. Even though a blister was starting to form on the small toe of his left foot and his clothing did little to slow the cold chill of the wind, he was enjoying himself. He was getting into that calm yet excited zone of pending action, those odd hours before you know the bullets are going to fly.

As an operator, he knew he must emotionally give himself to the mission. This is what he had trained for, prepared for in his mind. If he died during the operation, then it was just meant to be. Back in the teams they had used the phrase "Getting switched on", meat-eater vernacular for getting your head in the game. He was now "switched on".

He crossed the wide boulevard dodging several cars and trucks already seeing a line of attendees outside the beer hall's large front entrance. A heavy-set Brown Shirt SA officer in full uniform was walking down the growing line of people shouting commands. "Have your invitation in hand when you walk in the door. It will be checked…..Have your invitation in hand when you walk in the door. It will be checked."
Hauser stepped into line and surveyed the long cue of men ahead of him. It wasn't even six o'clock and already the crowd was in the hundreds. As the line slowly inched towards the hall's huge open double doors, he could see a thick knot of uniformed SA thugs at the entrance. They were indeed checking in close detail every invitation, weeding out those who did not have one and passing the ones who did. Suddenly a cold chill ran up his spine as he realized that the SA officers were frisking the attendees as they stepped up to the table. The men doing the searches were by no means professional in their methods, but they could get lucky and find the suppressed forty caliber and maybe even the return activator that hung around his neck. If that happened, the entire mission would be lost. The line was moving more quickly now. Soon he would be at the table. He would have to do something to divert attention and he needed to do it quickly.

He reached deep into his right coat pocket, his hand touching the pistol as he stepped closer to the table. He could feel rivulets of sweat running down his back even though it was forty degrees outside. *Think*, the voice screamed in his head. Suddenly, off to his right, a large flatbed truck loaded with barrels of beer turned the corner and made its way down the street towards the hall. Good strong German beer that would be tapped and served to the attendees was on its way. As if an answer to prayer, he recognized his opportunity.

As the truck rumbled by, he gripped the suppressed pistol and fired three quick shots through the lining of his pocket into the thick barrels less than thirty feet away. The sound of the truck engine, the Gentec suppressor, and the general street noise covered the shots as the rounds slammed into the heavy oak barrels, immediately sending a twenty foot white foaming geyser of beer into the air and onto the SA men by the door. Curses, shouts, and laughter filled the street as the Brown Shirts danced away from the exploding spray, desperately trying not to get their boots and uniforms wet. Several men stepped out of line to watch the confusion as the truck was stopped, the driver dragged out from behind the wheel, and confronted by several of the door guards.

This was his chance, he thought, stepping up to the table. He quickly handed his invitation to the distracted guard and smiled. The guard stamped the paper as he looked past him to see his men dealing with the hapless truck driver. "Next" he shouted, as he waved him through. Hauser stuffed the paper into his pocket and, with a sigh of relief, walked through the tall thick double doors of the massive hall. He was in.

****

It had been twenty harrowing hours since Clark had killed Pell and stuffed the body in the trunk of his rental car. As he sat in seat 4B on the last leg of his trip to the States from

Sydney, he let the tray table down and started spreading out the contents of Pell's wallet and other items taken from his pockets. It was the first time since the encounter with the over-confident agent that he had taken time to really look at what Pell had been carrying.

Clark thought back to the night's events. Before putting the body in the trunk, he went through the man's pockets and removed the wallet, ID case, cell phone, and a room key for the island's Loumaile Lodge Hotel. After sliding into the driver's seat, he turned on Pell's cell phone and in the dim light from the screen read the room number on the key... #23. Minutes later, he headed north on Lua Lulea Ave, driving as carefully as he could. A sudden rainstorm, which was all too common for this time of year, pounded down.

Driving through the nearly deserted streets, he found his windshield wipers could barely keep up with the lashing rain. *Christ*, he thought, turning on the car's defroster in a weak attempt to clear the windshield. Things had turned bad, really bad in seconds. Less than an hour before, he had just been a man on the run, a nobody in the grand scheme of things, a guy just trying to stay out of the line of fire until he could figure it all out.

It was then that he recognized that he had become a killer, a man no better than any of the hundreds of other killers and malcontents he had put away during his active tenure in the FBI. He could no longer stand back with a cold eye and emotional smugness and critically judge by the standards of the law another man for committing murder. That professional part of him died the microsecond he had blown Pell's head apart, creating heavy collateral damage.

He remembered pulling into the Loumile Lounge Hotel parking lot, finding a spot at the far west end. He backed in, his rear bumper coming to rest against the thick six-foot high Hibiscus hedge that framed the lot. Rain fell hard as he quickly wiped down the steering wheel and interior of the car, walked across the dimly lit lot, and ducked under the outside stairway of the hotel's second floor. He paused on the landing, scanning the area for movement. The place had been quiet, the rain keeping everyone inside, something that helped him. Hopefully no one had seen him drive Pell's rental car into the lot.

He found Pell's room and standing there in the dark in the room of the man he had just murdered, a cool shiver ran down his back. The sensation held him in place even though his mind had been screaming for him to move as fast as he could. He knew he had risked everything in coming to the hotel. If anyone had seen him drive in or, worse, seen him go into Pell's room, it would have created an easy connection for the police. He flipped on the wall light switch and quickly scanned the room.

Evidently Pell traveled light. A single medium size suitcase and a black leather computer briefcase lay on top of the bed. The suitcase was unlocked, inside, a couple of sport shirts, some shorts, running shoes, underwear, and several books about sailing. There was nothing that could point to what Pell did for a living, only the normal personal items of someone living in the mundane grooves that most of the population lived in. He quickly checked the rest of the room and, finding it devoid of anything else of informational value, he grabbed the computer bag and stepped back out into the night, closing the door behind him. The rain had stopped, leaving the air cool and clean. Refreshing… familiar.

He made his way across the still quiet parking lot and on to the deserted wet street. A half-mile down the road, he potted several taxies in front of a small bar, the music inside thumping out into the predawn. Walking up, he nodded to the sleepy-eyed driver of the first cab and slid into the back seat.

"Where to brodda?" questioned the man as he checked him in the rear view mirror.

Clark handed him a hundred dollar bill. "Airport."

"You got it, man." The driver cranked down the meter arm and slowly eased out of the lot as he turned up his car radio.

Later that morning, at the airport, Clark paid cash for his ticket as he tried to keep his rising fear and apprehension under control. He knew that Pell's body probably wouldn't be discovered for at least eight hours, maybe longer. Through basic police work, he knew they would eventually learn that he had been the last person to see Pell alive. The desk clerk at his hotel would remember the fight, and the link would be made.

Now, as he sat looking at Pell's possessions on the tray, he could still not find a discernable reason for why he had killed the man in the first place. He never thought of himself as someone who could commit cold murder. He had been convinced that he would never be able to cross that boundary.

If the Kingdom wanted his head for the limited knowledge he carried about *Stone Gate*, having executed one of their own would only amplify the wrath already headed his way. As the older blond stewardess, who had been a beauty in her youth, handed him his third rum and coke of the flight, he knew he could not run fast enough or fly far enough away to stay alive more than another week or two. The world had become a very small place. The Kingdom had total reach. There would be more Pells. There would be more government-sanctioned assassins, those who would relish the chance to kill him as those actions would guarantee a move up in the food chain of operators. Dark side wet work always brought tangible rewards.

As he sipped his drink, staring flatly out the window of the plane, he felt a strange emotional pull on his heart, a yearning, or better defined - a desire to be in a place he had never been before. When he thought back to when the odd feelings had begun, New Mexico immediately came to mind. That day, in that dusty, nearly deserted housing project, it had all begun. The second he had walked up to the burned-out ruins of Doctor Taylor's lab and stared down into that strange, yet terrifying blue white light in the bottom of the pit, his life changed. He had refused to admit up until now that he was somehow connected to the anomaly; it was drawing him closer, pulling him across time and space for reasons he still did not understand.

He downed the last of his drink and motioned for the stewardess to bring him another, knowing full well that no matter how much of the body numbing liquor he drank, it would never dull the rising terror of seeing the anomaly again. Never.

In three hours his plane would be landing in Canada, and the final leg of his journey would begin. With luck, he would live long enough to see most of it. Then again he had no illusions of any prolonged survival. The deck was heavily stacked. Everyone knows that the house always wins. Bullets and brains can only take a man so far. Fate always takes a deep cut, no matter how hard you play.

Chapter Seven

Hauser steadied his breathing as he made his way across the already crowded beer hall to the bar at the far side of the room. There was tangible electricity in the air, the expectant crowd in a near frenzy of excitement. Surveying the crowd with his back against the bar, he knew that the moment he made the shot he would have to initiate the return device. There would be no second chances.

During his extensive mission training at Langley, his handlers had told him repeatedly that they still did not have a clear idea what would happen to the space-time Continuum the moment he killed the man he was after. A hundred million people had been directly affected by the war, a war he was about to stop before it even began.

Theories had been presented in the briefings. Some considered that nothing would happen, that events were in parallel with time and would simply take another course or outcome from the new reality. Other more ominous predictions postulated that because of the massive disruption to known history and this current reality, all time would stop and the universe as he knew it would collapse in a nanosecond. Others said that the killing would cause a dimensional shift, creating a totally different world for all involved. The one thing that was a constant: things would change the second he pulled the trigger and the life that he knew and loved would never be the same. *Nothing like having the weight of the known universe resting on whatever action you take.*

Clark knew if he really thought of the staggering consequences connected to what he was about to attempt, he might simply drink his beer, watch the macabre Nazi spectacle, and then leave the hall without doing what he had traveled through time and space to do. No, to do this right, he knew he had to shut down every emotional link to his past and personality, things and events in his life that had shaped and molded him into the man he was now. He had to "switch on" and give himself over to the greater cause, accepting the fact that he was already dead. It was an emotional ledge few men could walk next to, a lofty, lonely place reserved only for true believers.

He watched as hundreds more uniformed Brown Shirted SA men filed into the hall, falling into ranks from the front of the large stage that had been set up to the back of the room. To his surprise, he became aware that only a few men in attendance were in civilian clothes like himself, a fact that began to raise his anxiety level even more. A man in street clothes moving through the crush of uniformed soldiers no longer blended in. Hiding in plain sight was becoming more difficult by the minute.

The seemingly endless procession of SA continued to pour in from the street as Hauser sipped the last of his beer. It was now becoming evident that he would not be allowed anywhere near Hitler when he finally walked into the hall to speak. The men in civilian clothes were being asked to move to the balcony or to the back of the room. Hauser nodded to the sweaty, moon-faced officer who had pointed upstairs and slowly followed several other men towards the short steep balcony staircase.

For Hauser, the room now carried a hostile, barely controlled edge, the kind of bad vibe found in the crowded south-of-the-border bars, whorehouses, and over crowded jails, places where you kept your head on a swivel and your body ready for a fight. All of the SA were armed with pistols and knives and carried the same "fuck you" swagger of every hard core thug and low-life Hauser had ever run across, the kind of unearned false power street-scum get when they join a gang and are given a weapon.

Making his way into the large balcony, he counted no less than eight film crews, their large tripod cameras set up side by side just behind the arched top rail of the loft. Lights were being set up, and the crews seemed to be working at a fevered pitch, not wanting to miss the shot when the man of the hour made his grand entrance. Looking over the rail at the rank and file below, Hauser estimated at least three hundred men stood in shoulder-to-shoulder ranks.

Scanning the room, he estimated that it would be a solid forty-yard shot from where he stood on the balcony rail down to the stage. It would be a long shot with a pistol and nearly impossible with subsonic ammunition, ammunition that had been specifically designed for the weapon he carried, and more importantly, made to deliver a sledgehammer hit close up, not from forty to fifty yards. He was a world-class marksman with a handgun, but delivering a fatal headshot to a target that was five foot eight and a hundred and sixty pounds at that distance would be a stretch for any professional shooter. Cigarette and cigar smoke hung heavy in the air. That, along with the heat of four hundred people jammed into a poorly ventilated hall, was beginning to make this an even more uncomfortable, stifling affair. Sweat was now running down the middle of his back. A tension headache had started to push its way from one side of his head to the other.

Jesus, it's hot up here, he thought, quickly unbuttoning the top three buttons of his shirt. His weapon was in his overcoat pocket, which meant it would be impossible to take it off. The few open seats behind him in the gallery were quickly filling up, pushing him toward a decision on what he had to do next. Soon there would only be standing room in the balcony, and the idea of standing butt to nut in the sweltering darkness while his target railed away for hours down below seemed insufferable.

He was already feeling the heat-induced nausea roll up from his gut, and the last thing he needed was to pass out, drawing even more attention to himself. He had to move now, had to get out of the suffocating heat. As he pushed his way past the men coming up the stairs, he considered for a moment that he might not make it. Several of the men he shoved past had thrown elbows into his ribs, actions that in any other circumstance would have sparked a fist-throwing melee. Now, all he desperately wanted to do was get out of the building and into the fresh air.

Finally getting to the main floor, he pushed his way through the last few SA members who were coming in and with the last of his strength, bolted through the large double doors, vomiting his breakfast in a strong yellow stream onto the sidewalk. Seconds later, several SA soldiers jerked him to his feet and shoved him farther into the street, shouting and kicking. Evidently, throwing up at the entrance, the entrance through which Fuehrer would pass, was frowned upon by the guards.

Hauser now found himself in a full-blown fistfight with three of the men, all desperately trying to land solid punches and kicks. The fight moved across the street and into the open park on the other side, the men trying to keep their footing on the wet grass. Hauser side-kicked one of his attackers in the chest, sending him to the ground with a groan. The other two dove into him, throwing wild punches that he quickly deflected. His Krav Maga training was now kicking in as he deftly blocked, countered and then knocked both men to the ground. He looked across the street and saw another pack of uniformed SA running his way. Seeing that he had already drawn way too much attention to himself, he took off in a sprint in the opposite direction hoping to put as much distance from himself and the SA as possible.

Less than a block farther the shouts and sounds of pursuit faded into the early evening traffic noise. At least ten blocks away from the beer hall, he quickly ducked into one of the brightly lit cafés. He needed to check the damage and collect himself before he made his next move. After ordering a cup of coffee from the pretty girl behind the counter, he found a quiet table near the back of the café. *Christ*, he thought wiping a small bit of blood from his nose with his sleeve. *What the hell had just happened?* With hands trembling from adrenaline, he took a sip of the strong brew, still not believing the raw truth of what had just taken place. He had choked, freaked out, got the yips right when he needed everything to be online.

For the first time in his life he had experienced a full-blown panic attack, something he had scoffed at before when others had had them. He had considered them to be weak when they had faltered with similar reactions, chalked it up to having a soft spot in character, a non-hacker, someone labeled in military jargon as "Unsat."
Consciously slowing his breathing, he now realized that he had blown the mission, missed his chance at doing what he had come to do. His mind was a blur as the waitress walked up and asked him if he wanted more coffee, "Yes, bitta" he replied holding up his cup. Collecting himself, he began to check his pockets to see if he had lost any gear in the fight. Relieved to see that his weapon was still buried deep in his coat pocket, he reached under his shirt for the small square plastic return device that he wore around his neck. A jolt of sudden panic flashed through his body as he discovered the chain and the device were gone.

As if his body were covered with ants, he furiously padded and searched his clothes for the device. He stood up and shook the legs of his pants, desperately hoping that the small box was still on his body somewhere. He was almost in tears as he slumped back into his chair. The cold realization that he had lost the one thing he needed to get back home fell on him like a cold rain. Not only had he failed his mission, he was now stuck in 1939 in prewar Germany. Short of getting killed, this was the worst possible outcome. As things were now, his only options were to wait until the beer hall meeting was over, go back and see if he could see where he had dropped the device, or accept the fact that the device was lost and deal with the fact that his past was just that - his past. In that case he would have to leave the area, create a new life, a new reality. Little did he know that at that very moment, the decision of what to do next was already being made for him. Fate had stepped in and was calling the shots.

Chapter Eight

As he did every night just before midnight since he had been put in charge of the project, Shaw was in his office going over the day's data, checking all of the information that had been coming in on a steady feed. They had a man down range running one of the most important missions yet devised, and nothing could be left to chance. Stone Gate and everything associated with it was the most carefully protected and monitored operation since the Manhattan Project.

Scientists worked around the clock, insuring constant access to the Continuum, monitoring and controlling the enormous energy needs and the monumental quantum mechanics of operational time travel. In addition, most of the relatable core energy for the phasing operations was controlled by a medium sized fusion reactor, an eight-gig, high energy world-ender located two buildings over from the lab on 18th Street in Crystal City. The highly secured underground facility was also manned and operated on a twenty-four/seven basis by a team of physicists, security specialists, and Kingdom liaison supervisors. The NSA ran the machine. The Kingdom ran the show.

There would be riots in the streets if the average commuting Washingtonian suddenly found out that for years they had been walking and driving directly over an extremely powerful and experimental fusion reactor fifty-eight feet below them. If only they knew that this machine was part of the mechanism responsible for controlling and changing lives, but only a select few had knowledge of its existence. Funding for the operation had been on the dark side soon after Doctor Taylor's discovery in Albuquerque two years earlier. None of the money needed was ever discussed in any appropriations committee meetings, nor was it discussed as part of the

Senate's yearly Intelligence budgetary line items. The funds
were simply allocated on direct vendor drafts requested by
the NSA, a wet dream process for the dark side shot callers
running Stone Gate.

Just as Shaw was about to wrap it up for the night, his desk
phone rang jarring him from his late night fatigue. "Yeah,
what's up?" he asked easing back in his chair.

"Sir, ah, you need to get down here. We have a situation,"
replied the phasing room team lead, the tension in his voice
barely under control. Shaw immediately hung up the phone
and hurried out of his office. Whatever had put the yips into
the team lead had come through in the man's voice.
Something bad was happening eighty feet down the corridor,
and he needed to get there.

Quickly swiping his proximity card through the reader, he
pushed his way through the heavy steel doors of the lab and
was immediately met by an armed NSA security officer. "This
way, sir," he announced, trotting back through the lab. Shaw
was stunned to see that the officer had his weapon drawn as
he followed him towards the phasing room. Easing up to the
doors of the second lab, the officer nodded to Shaw and then
pushed his way through.

Once inside, Shaw was stunned to see a man standing
between the return array panels holding a pistol, shouting in
German. "Voss is los?" He screamed at the four NSA security
officers pointing their weapons at him. The man looked as if
he was about to cry as he stared wide-eyed at the security staff
and scientists standing nearby.

"Lower your weapons!" shouted Shaw stepping forward.
"Everyone, calm down." Shaw could see that the man was in
deep distress sobbing softly and trembling as if he was
freezing. Shaw stepped closer, his hands raised. "It's okay," he

whispered.

Terrified, the man raised his weapon. "Zuruckbe Kommen!" he shouted stepping back. "Zuruckbe Kommen!"

"Anybody speak German?" questioned Shaw looking around the room.

"Yes, sir," replied one of the scientists standing nearby. "He's telling you to get back."

Shaw nodded to the man and stepped back, his hands still raised. "Okay, no problem. Everybody back up."

"Sir, that's a bad idea, we need to… "

"Quiet," interrupted Shaw. "I want everybody out of the room."

"Sir, I don't…"

"Now!" shouted Shaw. "Everybody out, goddamn it. Now!"

As the men slowly stepped out of the lab, Shaw kept eye contact with the trembling visitor. "It's okay," he said softly trying to ease the tension. "It's all right." The man seemed to relax a bit as the last technician left the lab, his attention fully on Shaw.

"Voss is los?' he questioned, his voice barely a whisper.

Shaw slowly lowered his hands, his mind a blur. It was bad enough that the man was armed and deeply distraught, but more stunning - he was not the SEAL they had sent into the Continuum. Instead, he was a German stranger wearing a brown shirt, Nazi uniform, armband swastika and all. "My God," whispered Shaw. "My God."

****

Twenty three hundred miles to the northwest, Clark's plane, a 747 wide body was on final approach into Vancouver International. It had been an easy flight, one that had given him time to think about his next move. He knew that the minute he cleared customs they would stop him. It would either be there or shortly after he cleared the terminal. His only way of escape was to use the Medallions Costa had given him just before he left the Vatican. He knew the Medals worked, having been a witness to their astonishing powers while at the police station in Coloma, Michigan, when he first picked them up.

It had been a routine assignment by the Art Crimes Unit of the FBI, a unit he had been assigned to after the Albuquerque incident. His instructions had been clear. Pick up the Medallions and bring them back to the FBI in DC. Simple. Yet, nothing about the recent strange and deadly turns in his life had been simple. In the span of three weeks, he had violated every professional oath he had ever taken, killed a man he did not know and was now getting ready to use a priceless religious artifact to help secure his freedom. He tried not to speculate on what the next three weeks might bring. If he was going to make a move, now was the time to do it. People in the plane were now involved in the general confusion of standing and working at getting their luggage out of the overhead bins. He quickly got out of his seat, pulled the small backpack out of the overhead, and slowly pushed his way through the crowded aisle.

Relieved to see that both restrooms were unoccupied, he opened one of the doors and stepped inside the tiny space. Breathing a sigh of relief, he locked the door behind him and pulled the Silver Medal out of his backpack. Holding up the Medallion, he was in awe of how really strikingly beautiful it was. The detailed engraving and silver chain sparkled in the clear, unforgiving florescent light of the bathroom. Closing his eyes and taking a deep breath, he quickly draped the chain around his neck, immediately feeling the heavy medal suck down against his chest. Slowly he opened his eyes and looked in the mirror above the small sink. A jolt of fear ripped through his body as he gasped. He could now see the back wall of the tiny restroom in the mirror, yet his image was gone. He was invisible.

****

The SA soldier had calmed a bit after the room had cleared, giving Shaw a chance to slowly pull up a lab stool and sit down. In the back of the lab near the large entrance door, the scientist who said he spoke German quietly eased into the room and stepped up beside Shaw. "Thought you might need an interpreter, sir," he said softly, his eyes fixed on the man holding the pistol.

Shaw nodded. "Good, very good. Ask him if he has any idea how he got here."

The scientist motioned to the man. "Wie sind Sie hier her gekommen?" he questioned in German.

The soldier shook his head. "Ich weiß nicht."

"He has no idea, sir. What else would you like for me to ask him?"

Shaw thought for a moment. "Ask him if he can remember what he did right before showing up here."
"Woran erinnern Sie sich zuletzt?"

The soldier thought for a moment as a look of fearful confusion clouded his face. "Ich habe etwas gefunden."

"He said he found something," announced the scientist.

"Okay," replied Shaw. "Ask him what he found and where."

"Was haben Sie zu finden und wo ?" questioned the aide.

The soldier lowered his pistol slightly. "Ein kleines Feld in der Straße."

The scientist nodded. "He said it was a box he found in the street."

Shaw held up both hands and smiled at the soldier. "Tell him he is safe here and that we can help him," he said calmly. "He can put the gun down."

The scientist cleared his throat. "Du bist sicher hier aus können Sie die Waffe DOWN."

The soldier held a steady gaze. "Wie bin ich hier , und wer bist du Menschen ?" he questioned calmly.

The aid leaned close to Shaw. "He wants to know who we are and how he got here."

Shaw slowly slid off the lab stool and pointed to the ID badge that hung around his neck. "Tell him I am Doctor Shaw and that he was brought here by mistake. Tell him that we will do everything we can to fix what has happened. He has to trust us."

The aid nodded and stepped closer. "Ich bin, Doktor Shaw, und das war ein Fehler, wir werden Sie hep, müssen Sie uns vertrauen."

The soldier thought for a moment and then slowly holstered his pistol, his eyes locked on Shaw. "Okay, aber ich halte meine Waffe ."

The aid nodded. "Sir, he said okay, but he is keeping his weapon."

Shaw smiled and nodded at the soldier. "Okay, that's a start."

Chapter Nine

Clark stood quietly in the plane's bathroom a solid ten minutes after hearing the flight crew and pilots leave. Confident that he was finally alone, he slowly opened the collapsible door and stepped out. It was the strangest feeling, moving down the aisle of the now deserted 747, the air still heavy with the smell of body odor, coffee, and all the scents that linger after a fifteen-hour flight. He welcomed the cool and fresh air as he stepped onto the jet way on his way to customs and the terminal. Up ahead, at the end of the long entryway, stood four sets of glass doors that had large red letters in both English and French: CUSTOMS, HAVE YOUR PASSPORTS READY. As he stood trying to figure out how to trigger the sensor to open the doors, several members of a cleaning and catering crew pushed their way through from the other side.

For a second he forgot he was invisible and started to explain why he was on the other side of the glass. To his shock, the three women quickly bustled by with their vacuums and buckets without even a glance. *Unreal*, he whispered to himself as the cleaning crew disappeared up the jet way. Taking a deep breath he quickly turned and stepped through the glass doors just before they closed behind him. After walking down a brightly lit hallway, he stepped down a short flight of stairs into an expansive room that could easily accommodate a thousand people. At the far end stood a line of small glass enclosed boxes, stations manned by CBSA, *Canadian Border Security Agency* officers.

Looking around the room, he realized that the only way out was past one of the kiosks. Fortunately, the only doors he would have to go through were a short distance behind the check-in boxes, doors that were being opened and closed on a regular basis by cleared passengers on their way to baggage claim. He stepped into the back of one of the shortest lines and slowly made his way, being careful not to get close to a man in shoulder length dreadlocks who had no idea that he was behind him.

After several minutes, he was at the kiosk and then past it on his way to the large set of automatic doors that led into the terminal. Dreadlocks who seemed to be bored with the whole affair, carrying himself in a way that projected his "coolness", was walking at an annoyingly slow pace. He finally tripped the sensor that opened the doors. Irritated by having to wait on the slacker, Clark stepped up close behind him and in a hushed voice whispered "Dumbass."

As if he had been punched in the head, Dreadlocks spun away from the voice so quickly that he fell to the floor, losing both his grungy flip-flops and his backpack in the process. Wide-eyed, he slowly got to his feet, desperately looking for the thing or person who had whispered in his ear.

God, this is fun, thought Clark walking past the man. It was amazing how powerful he felt. As he walked away he decided to give Dreadlocks a parting shot and shouted over his shoulder, "Get a haircut, freak." Clark smiled as he watched Dreadlocks run by as if he were on fire, leaving his flip-flops behind. *So far, so good.*

****

"What do you mean he was *not* on the airplane?" shouted Mike Pryor, the Deputy Security Director. He was at his desk listening to the field agent on the secure line. "You need to explain to me how someone can get on a 747 in Sydney, fly fifteen hours, and then vanish before landing in Canada. How is that possible, Agent Frost?"
"Sir, we tracked Agent Clark in Sydney, saw him get on the airplane, and when the plane landed in Vancouver, he was not on it. I cannot explain it.'"

Pryor eased back in his chair, trying to get his anger under control. He hated operational failures like this. Clark was a loose end, one that needed to be tied up as quickly as possible. The shot callers expected results, and it was a black mark on his record if those results were not achieved. Failure did not play well at the Kingdom.

"All right, Agent Frost, here's what's going to happen. Get as many people as you need to recheck both departing and arrival points on Clark's trip. Interview anyone you have to. Find his seat number and get a DNA swab to verify he even got on the goddamned airplane in the first place. Check every contact Clark has had for the last five years and see if he has reached out to any of them. Find this guy, Frost, and find him quick. Failure is not an option. As long as he is above ground he is a threat to the security of the United States. Do you need any more clarification on this?"

"No, sir."

"All right, find this son-of-a-bitch and end it. I will not be happy if I get another one of these phone calls."

"Yes, sir. I understand, Sir. Concerning Agent Pell's body, the Tongales authorities have refused to release it. What are your instructions?"

"Don't worry about it. State Department paperweights are going through the normal back channels on that. You stay focused on Clark. He has no money that we know of, no support, and nowhere to hide. This should not be that difficult."
"Yes, sir."

"I want this thing wrapped up within the week. Clear?"

"Yes, sir. We're on it."

"Counting on it, Agent. Keep me posted." Before Frost could answer, Pryor disconnected the call. He saw little need for further chitchat. Sitting back in his chair, he tried to think of what else could be done to bring this latest situation to a quick close. According to Clark's file there was nothing extraordinary about him or his background. His career with the FBI had been stunningly normal, at least until he had come across Stone Gate. After that, he had been de-programmed, broken, and then transferred to the Art Crimes unit in DC, a backwater, dead end assignment where he could be monitored and corrected if the need arose. If it had been left up to him, Clark would have been eliminated the moment he stepped out of the Albuquerque facility. Why he had he been left alive was a mystery. Many others had been taken out for a fraction of what Clark had been exposed to.

It did not make sense, unless it was supposed to be this way. Maybe the grey beards that were really calling the shots for Stone Gate wanted Clark to survive, needed him to do something. He let the supposition hang in the air. Whatever the brass had decided one way or another was way above his pay grade, and as any good and loyal soldier, he would follow orders and make sure FBI Agent Clark was dead by the end of the week.

He had been dealing in the commodity of death in the nation's interest for years now. Even as an 06 Marine Officer, he had been hip deep in the real blood sport of sending men into harm's way. Three tours in Iraq with the 5th Marines had given him the chance to see it up close, close enough to feel his own fragile mortality that cold windy afternoon in late 2008 while heading down Route Irish out of Baghdad. His Hummer and three others just like it had set off an IED daisy chain of five 105-howitzer rounds, an ambush that shredded the convoy and ten other SOTG Marines that were with him.

He barely survived the year at Walter Reed, and the day he walked out under his own power eleven months and seven surgeries later he had been approached by a head hunter from the ultra secret intelligence organization called *"The Kingdom."*

The Kingdom was the name high level government security and dark side intelligence operatives had given the organization that had been formed under the Truman Administration. For decades the power and influence of the Kingdom had grown dramatically, extending its reach far beyond the imagination of its originators. NSA, CIA, and the DIA all fed information, manpower, equipment and support to the Kingdom, along with a core group of influential Congressional "Advisors", who made sure, through restricted black budget hearings, that the money still flowed. The Kingdom was the real power behind the curtain. Presidents came and went, some, if not most, had not even been read into the ongoing operations of the organization, having been deemed untrustworthy, weak, and not the kind of men who could carry that kind of operational power.

Even the current President was not allowed access to any of the Kingdom's operations because of his subversive "social justice" ideology and unpopular sympathies for countries and forces hostile to the United States. His almost total exclusion from the Kingdom and the Stone Gate operation in particular was never a question. He would be allowed to play his four to eight years of social manipulation games, but the real power and influence came from a select few, from men whose offices were in several nondescript buildings in downtown Washington DC. Self-promoting politicians came and went, along with their policies and misguided views of the world. The Kingdom never wavered in its position of control…never.

****

Hauser let another hour go by, still trying to figure out what his next move should be. The young waitress had filled his coffee cup twice now and, in Hauser's mind, was starting to get far too comfortable with him being there. The last thing he needed now was to be memorable to anyone. Now resigned to the fact that he had to go back to the beer hall and try and find the device that could get him home, he left a Duetsh Mark on the table and nodded to the barmaid on his way out. Stepping out onto the sidewalk, he pulled his collar tight as a cold gust of rain-soaked wind blew down the street. Vehicle traffic was still heavy in spite of the gloom and rain.

As Hauser walked, he thought about his father and how proud he had been of him when he graduated from BUDS a lifetime ago. He wondered what the old man would think of him now. He hadn't thought about that day in years and was surprised that the memory had resurfaced. His parents had driven all the way from Great Falls, Montana to California just to see him get the Trident. Looking back, it had been one of the best days of his life. As he continued to walk, a sudden unexpected stab of pain hit him just above the heart as he recalled the death of his mother less than two weeks after the graduation. She had been working in her garden when a brain aneurysm had taken her from them. She had been only 64 years old. Her sudden death had rocked the family, scaring his father with a grief he carried to this day; some wounds were just too deep to heal.

He shook the memory and focused in on the crowd of men and cars under the streetlights across the avenue in front of the beer hall. The event appeared to be breaking up as more and more people walked out through the large double doors and onto the sidewalk. Even from where he stood on the other side of the street, he could smell the odor of cheap cigars, cigarette smoke, and stale beer rolling out of the hall.

A raucous crowd now filled the street, men who had been stirred by the speaker. Hauser knew that this was the most dangerous time to be here. The attendees had become charged with a fiery rhetoric, fueled by beer and a long suppressed urge of Germans to right the wrong of the odious Versailles Treaty following the First World War. It had been a treaty that forced war reparations on a beaten population, a population that could not even feed itself, much less pay a crushing debt, a debt that had bankrupted the country and put millions out onto the street.

In his speeches, Hitler had captured the population's rage, channeling the pain of defeat and promising a new path. He had been able to turn the punishment into a cause. The "world" was doing this to Germany. The people had been betrayed, sold out by sycophants and liars, men without honor, a ruling class that needed to be rooted out and destroyed. Then and only then could the greatness of Germany be re-stored. As Hauser walked past the men with blood in their eyes, he could see how easy it had been for Hitler to set the world on fire. Hate was a powerful a weapon.

Chapter Ten

Shaw carefully handed the man the Styrofoam cup of coffee as the two sat across from one another at one of the lab tables. The SA man kept his pistol on the table, a provision he was not willing to concede. Shaw nodded to the lab assistant who was interpreting German. "Ask him if he would like a cigarette."

The assistant thought a moment. "Okay, ah, Mochten Sie Eine Zigarette?"

"Nein," replied the man shaking his head. "Warum ist das so cup Licht?" he asked holding up the cup of coffee.

The assistant smiled. "Sir, he wants to know why the cup is so light."

Shaw picked up his own cup. "Tell him it's made of a new kind of paper." It never occurred to Shaw that a man in prewar Germany would not know what Styrofoam was. He could only guess at the level of mental dislocation the SA officer was experiencing.

Even some of the men who had been prepped, trained for months prior to moving through the Continuum, had severe emotional problems upon their return. On the "cost side" of Stone Gate there were men who had suffered mental breakdowns; others had committed suicide, all considered necessary "Data points" for future Stone Gate missions. Shaw had often wondered what the family members of these men thought had happened to their love ones when they returned after participating in a "Classified Government Operation." Many of the real meat-eaters who had once been at the top of their game within the Special Operations community, the cool guys, the PT freak alpha males that made it all look so easy were crippled wolves that now haunted the crowded halls of emergency rooms and mental institutions. They had been fed willingly into the machine and then brought back, in some cases deeply scarred and emotionally disturbed, injuries that no amount of therapy or drugs could cure.

The man had calmed considerably since his unexpected arrival and now sat staring at Shaw with a mixture fear and suspicion. "Wo bin ich und wie bin ich hierher gekommen?" he asked tapping the table.

"He wants to know where he is and how he got here," replied the assistant.

Shaw leaned back in his chair with a sigh. "Okay, all right. I want you to translate exactly what I say."

"Yes, sir."

"Tell him it's not so much *where* but *when*. He is now in the year 2015. The small box he found was a device that allows time travel. In the future, his future, scientists discover how to move through the space-time Continuum. When he pushed the button on that box, he was transferred though the Continuum and ended up here, in the future. Tell him we are the ones who control this process."

"Sir, do you think that's wise?" he asked softly. "I mean, he is a Nazi. Do we really owe him an explanation?"

"He's a human being," replied Shaw. "Our device brought him here, so we *do* have a responsibility to give him an honest explanation. If you have a problem with that, I will find someone else to help me talk to this man."
"No, sir, I mean yes, sir," nodded the assistant.

As he began tell the man in German what Shaw had just said, Shaw watched the man's expression turn from suspicion to open mouth shock. When the assistant had finished, the man shook his head. "Das ist nicht möglich, " he whispered.

"He said this is impossible," replied the assistant.

Shaw thought for a moment and then stood up slowly. "Tell him I want to show him something. Tell him he can bring his weapon if he puts it in his holster. No harm will come to him."

"Ich habe etwas, um Ihnen zu zeigen , können Sie Ihre Waffe zu nehmen, wenn Sie es Halfter. Kein Schaden wird zu Ihnen kommen."

The man locked eyes with Shaw, looking for the lie. Seeing none, he stood up and holstered the pistol.

In the two years since Stone Gate had become fully operational, Shaw had been the facilitator for other men in their opportunities to travel through time. He had been the wizard behind the curtain making sure the process of changing the world went according to plan. He had interviewed at length every man who had been sent back and returned, astonished by the reports and rich experiences.

Shaw couldn't help but envy their opportunities. No matter how well he facilitated the program or how efficient he was with the Stone Gate budget, he would not be on the roster for future operations. His superiors had deemed him too valuable to the program, too vital to risk. Being the lead Program Manager for Stone Gate was an honor he did not take lightly, yet knowing that he would never experience the life changing sensations of being carried through the Continuum bothered him greatly. Now, through no effort of his own, a piece of living history had appeared from the past, giving him a taste of the time travel experience. As he walked down the lab's corridor, he still did not have a clear idea of how he was going to deal with the German. The man was not some abstract theory or some figure in a second hand story told by another but was a living, breathing, a very much *alive* human being. He would have family, people who cared about him, connections to his time, his reality. Shaw was very much aware of the fact that he was now moving in uncharted waters. Sending people back in time was one thing; bringing someone from the past was another. The possible implications were staggering.

Shaw pushed through the last set of Mag-lock doors that opened into a large reception area and security station. Four armed NSA Security enforcement agents stood at the far entrance keeping anyone else from entering the cleared room. "It's okay, fellas," announced Shaw, seeing the men react to a uniformed and armed man stepping into the room. He watched as they slowly recognized the Brown Shirt Nazi regalia.

Shaw walked over to the large set of windows that looked down onto the building's parking lot. "Tell him, I'd like him to look out the window."

The assistant nodded to Shaw and then spoke to the German. "Bitte schauen Sie aus dem Fenster."

The German slowly walked over to the window and looked down onto the lot. "Ask him if he has ever seen cars like those down there."

The assistant stepped up close to the window. "Haben Sie überhaupt Fahrzeuge wie die gesehen?
The man stared down onto the lot in utter amazement. "Mein Gott," he whispered. All the different colored Toyotas, Hondas and pickup trucks of the people who worked at the facility had to be a stunning sight to someone who had only

seen black vehicles his entire life.

"Tell him I have something else to show him," announced Shaw.

"Ich muss Sie etwas anderes zu zeigen." The man nodded and followed Shaw back across the room, through the double doors, and into the lab hallway. Shaw could only imagine what was going through the German's mind as he led the men into his office. He quickly sat down behind his desk and turned on his desktop computer. "Tell him this is a computer. I am going to let him see some things about Germany on it."

"Dies ist ein Computer, und ich möchte Ihnen etwas über Deutschland darauf , zu zeigen",

Shaw typed in the phrase *Post World War Germany* and then set the translation from English to German. Immediately a full menu of World War Two articles and subject headings popped up. He clicked on one that had video of the fall of Berlin. He then motioned for the man to sit and look at the screen. Like a scared child, the man slowly sat down and in stunned amazement watched as he saw the intense street warfare of the Russians storming the *Reich Chancellery.* The grainy black and white footage showed Red Army soldiers climbing over the ruble of the now destroyed Third Reich, the film ending with the iconic exploding giant bronze swastika. After a moment, with tears in his eyes, the German looked up at Shaw. "Wie kann das sein ?

"He's asking how can this be?" replied the assistant.

Shaw sat down on the edge of the desk, trying to think of what he should say. "Okay, tell him that Adolf Hitler started a world war in 1939 and, that Germany was defeated in June of 1945. Millions died."

The assistant pointed to the computer screen. "Adolf Hitler begann einen Weltkrieg im Jahre 1939 und wurde im Juni 1945 besiegt, millionen starben."

Shaw could see that the German was fighting a crushing emotional battle, desperately trying to hold on. It was a terrible thing to watch a man's hopes and beliefs, no matter how misguided, crumble and die right before your eyes.

Suddenly enraged, the German stood up and drew his pistol. "Das ist alles Lügen , das nicht möglich ist!" he shouted.

Caught off guard by the man's sudden outburst, the assistant stepped backward, stumbling over the office trashcan, falling into the corner of the room with a crash.

"He says it's all lies!" shouted the assistant, struggling to get to his feet. As if the air in the room was suddenly sucked out, Shaw watched in horror as the German spun in the assistant's direction and fired two quick shots, blowing a large piece of his skull and blood onto the wall behind him. Instantly the German seemed to explode from within, as heavy automatic weapons fire from outside the office door poured in.

Shaw tumbled back over the desk as more gunfire roared into the small office as the NSA security team blew the German apart. Seconds later deafened and disoriented, Shaw slowly got to his feet as the security team rushed in and roughly pulled him from the room into the hallway.

"Sir, are you injured?" shouted one of the security officers, his face inches away from Shaw's.

"I, ah , I don't think so," he replied, suddenly realizing that the blood he was wiping from his face was not his.

At that same instant, seven hundred and thirty miles due west on I-90, just outside of Cleveland, Ohio, a large white Ford Econoline van struck the Inner Belt bridge abutment at sixty-five miles an hour. The shattering impact sent glass, steel, and plumbing supplies over the rail of the bridge into the slow moving brown water of the Cuyahoga River a hundred and thirty feet below. Witnesses to the crash told officers on the scene that the van had not been driving erratically before the impact but had just drifted from the far right lane and without braking, slammed into the bridge railing. No driver was ever found, either in the vehicle or in the river below. The driver had simply vanished.

A registration check of the van revealed that it had been registered to a Donald Dietrich of Dietrich Plumbing supply in Cleveland, Ohio. Upon further investigation, the registered owner's address was found to be occupied by a Mrs. Tessie Wilson, an eighty-four year old widow who had never heard of Donald Dietrich or the plumbing company.

Of course none of this was known by the NSA security officers now loading the body of the German onto a stretcher inside Shaw's office. An hour later the identification papers were checked and the dead man carried the name of "Hans Dietrich." Found in his things were several small black and white photos, presumably of his wife and an infant son. The name, barely visible in ink on the back of the child's picture said "Donald, 1939."

Chapter Eleven

Just before he left the Vancouver terminal, Clark walked into the large airport restroom by the Hertz rental car counter, having been invisible for the good part of an hour now. He was amazed at the personal power he felt at being able to see and hear other people without being seen. The Medallion gave him the feeling of a predator among the sheep, an emotionally jarring sensation to say the least.

Experiencing a growing sense of expectation, an odd twinge deep in the gut telling him that he was getting closer to what he really wanted, what his soul really needed, he instinctively knew that the feeling had something to do with the anomaly and the staggering power it carried. As he stood in the stall, he allowed his mind to go back over what had happened to him when he first came in contact with Stone Gate. Even thinking of that name sent a bolt of panic and pain through his chest, a very real physical manifestation of the government's thorough *Re-education Program*.

This was the first time in days that he had opened the door and let the memories of that terrible two weeks drift out. They had broken him, taken something away that he could not replace with time or distance. Stone Gate had been used as a weapon, an emotional spike driven deep into all that he believed in and trusted. Whatever this thing was, it had taken everything from him - his job, his friends, and worst of all, his sureness of self. And yet, through all the pain and confusion of who he was and where he was going, he knew he was being drawn to the very thing that had nearly destroyed him.

Thinking back, he knew the government had sealed what was left of the open gap in the Continuum in a massive concrete and steel vault on top of where Doctor Taylor's house and basement had once stood. The ground and surrounding desert in that part of Albuquerque had been fenced off and deemed off limits five miles in every direction by the government. This was the place he had gone to when he first started to investigate the disappearance of Greg Gander, the professor from the University of Montana.

He knew that going back to a concrete slab would not get him the kind of information he was seeking. He had to go to the new power center, the place where all of Doctor Taylor's incredible discoveries had been taken. Somewhere within the heavily protected labyrinth of covert government operations in DC, Stone Gate now functioned. He still had Pell's computer and phone. Hacking into the information on these devices would most likely lead him to the very doors he was looking for. Pulling the Gold Medallion out of his backpack and looking at the Silver Medallion hanging around his neck, he knew that these would be the tools that would get him close to the project.

Suddenly, someone trying to open the stall door jarred him from his thoughts. "It's occupied," he said loudly, instantly realizing that to anyone on the outside, the stall looked empty.

"Ah, excuse me, sorry."

Clark listened, as the man behind the apology seemed to hesitate at the closed stall door and then walk away. *Another complication of being invisible*, he thought. He needed to get out of the restroom and not draw any further unwanted attention. That meant he needed to keep wearing the Medallion until he was well clear of the Terminal as it was almost certain that all the exits were under surveillance.

Several minutes later, sure that no one else was in the restroom, he opened the door of the stall and made his way back out to the front of the Terminal. Due to the heavy foot traffic of people coming from and going to flights, it was easy to get through the automatic doors that led out to the bus and cab stations. It felt good to be standing outside feeling the early fall chill in the air. Unfortunately there was no way he would be able to take either a cab or a bus at the terminal, leaving him with the only option of walking, and he needed to be miles away from the airport before risking visibility.

Years ago he had visited Vancouver while participating in a FBI conference, one of those hands across the border kind of deals post 9-11 with the RCMP. The three-day event had been held at the convention center downtown, blocks away from where he had been staying at the Metropolitan Hotel. He set his path in that direction. As he walked away from the airport, he was careful to keep his distance from the edge of the busy roadway out of fear of being hit by the cars and buses that whizzed by. Now he needed to eat and, most importantly he needed to rest.

The jet lag was really starting to hammer in as he trotted across the main street leading into the airport. He stepped over the guardrail of the road and slid on the wet grass down the steep slope to the bottom of the embankment. Nine miles away he could see the city of Vancouver. In the distance the tall buildings along the harbor glistened in the bright sunlight, the clear Canadian air amplifying the effect. As he walked, he knew he needed a good ten hours of sleep and a decent meal before he pushed on to Spokane. Once he got into the States he would use the Gold Medal and see if it really did allow him to fly.

Christ, he thought, as he stepped over another guardrail. If anyone had told him his life would have taken this kind of surreal turn a year ago, he would have laughed in his face. In his wildest dreams he could not have made this stuff up, not in a million years.

****

Hauser spent the better part of three hours scouring the street, the park, and the area of the fight looking without success for the return device. The rain that had soaked him to the skin had turned to a light snow, dropping a heavy hush and a deep chill over the city. Exhausted from his search and the cold, he stood under a dim streetlight desperately trying to think of what he should do next.

The device was lost which meant he was lost never to return to the life he once had. For the first time in years under the orange glow of the gaslights, he broke down and cried, not a wail of discontent or injury but from numbing frustration at failure. He had been given the chance for greatness yet failed at the critical hour. All the training, all the prep, and he had fallen short of the task. Now all he had left was a weapon, thirty rounds, two hundred Duetcsh Marks, and the wet clothes on his back. Looking up into the light, he had never felt more alone. *Hang on*, he whispered to himself, *you know how this ends*.

Quickly wiping away the tears, he blew his nose clear and spit. "Fuck this," he mumbled. "Suck it up, Frogman." He shook off the self-pity and the cold. *I'm good*, he thought walking towards the lights of town. He had money, he was not injured, and most importantly he knew the goddamned future, a fact that gave him a great advantage in the grand scheme of things. He may not have been able to shoot the son-of-a-bitch tonight, but he knew a war was coming and war was something he was good at. Somehow he would get back to the States and be part of the Greatest Generation. In spite of the cold, he smiled as he moved down the quiet avenue. Fate had been oddly kind, giving him a front row seat to one of the most important events in history. He knew he could still make a difference. He could still save lives. He could still influence the future.

Up ahead, in the glow of streetlights, the green and white Swan Hotel sign was barely visible through the falling snow. *That will work* he thought crossing the street. *Get out of the cold, get some food and a good night's sleep, and get on with plan B.* Like Master Chief Mixon on Team Five used to say, "The mission isn't over till you're dead and even then... keep pushing." *Goddamn right.*

****

Shaw had been on and off the phone most of the morning attempting to explain to his superiors what had happened concerning the shooting of the German. The conference calls had been edgy, tinged with barely veiled threats and passive aggressive "suggestions" concerning continued operations under his leadership. As he hung up the phone just before noon, he knew that this kind of incident would not be tolerated again. In fact he was very surprised he hadn't already been fired...or worse.

For now, he would be allowed to continue in his role, his main task - to conduct an extensive impact study and peripheral analysis of losing track of a human being from 2015 into the tough reality of prewar Germany 1939. He had been told to stay focused on the original mission and complete the operation. His orders were to send another assassin through the Continuum before the end of the month, a daunting task considering the first attempt took almost a year to plan and execute.

As the Government's machine continued to run, the walls of his office had already been cleaned, the bullet holes patched, and a cover story of a laboratory explosion was already being used to explain the death of the assistant to his relatives. A Kingdom forensics team working out of Bethesda had

"Corrected" the assistant's skull post mortem. The mechanism of injury needed to match the lab explosion story. When they finished with the body, no signs of a gunshot wound to the head would ever be detected.

As ordered, the German's body was incinerated into a fine ash at a classified facility near George Town University. A narrow, non-descript driveway off of West Road just wide enough for a modern day sedan led to an underground parking garage and a set of Mag-lock steel reinforced doors. To the passive observer it was just one more standard parking garage that provided space for the people who worked at the McDonough Arena, the large sports facility built in 1951. In reality, in 1995 a state of the art Rotary Kiln and large afterburner had been installed in the sub-basement of the building. The commercial grade system, capable of producing heat ranges exceeding 2200 degrees, was hot enough to turn a human body into powder in three and a half minutes. Due to the extreme high heat and a steady flow of pressurized oxygen into the burners, the exhaust turned into steam and water vapor that vented harmlessly into the air on the east side of the Arena. Over the years, countless Government "mistakes" had been corrected by the operations at McDonough. The German was just one more in a long line of mistakes.

Chapter Twelve

"So, in summary, Mike, we are unable to locate Agent Clark even though our people saw him get on the plane in Australia? And the asset we sent after Clark was found dead in the trunk of the rental car in Tonga? Is that pretty much the basic information so far?" Clay Crawford leaned back in his chair while lighting his pipe.

"That's correct, sir," replied Pryor. "I have two full teams on the ground in Canada and in Australia. We still do not know where Clark is or how he got off that 747."

Crawford thought for a moment while puffing his pipe, filling the room with the smell of strong cherry blend. "So, what are your expectations, Mike?" he asked flatly, a tone that both questioned and minimized at the same time.

This is where he had to be careful thought Pryor, shifting uneasily in his chair. He was sitting in the office of Clay Crawford, *the* Clay Crawford. Top of his class, Yale 51, Bones man, CIA section chief in Bangkok during Vietnam running all the wet work in the Highlands and the Delta with Special Forces MIKE teams, he had quickly gained a heavy rep of being the "go to guy' in Special Ops with the brass balls and the right DC connections if it all fell apart. He had a six million-piaster reward on his head by the NVA yet had enough sand to maintain a permanent suite in the Con Tien Hotel in Saigon for years. He drove his own beat-up Citron car from the DMZ to Cam Ron Bay armed with a .357 Mag with hot loads and a cut down M14 just to make it fun. He was *"that guy"*, the one who had that weird light around him when the scene really took a turn for the surreal. Rounds could be zipping through the compound, and he would be walking upright talking to the fast movers on the monster net for close air support knowing full well that he wasn't going to get a scratch. The man carried that heavy, crazy brave Karma that really wasn't crazy, just really smart. He was the guy men respected for his intelligence and guts but feared for his power.

After the war he had moved on to bigger and better things, climbing up through the company in the dark side work, but he had learned early on that the meat-eaters carrying the weapons, those really out in the bush, were not the ones who moved up the food chain. The shot callers in the DC Westside offices had the real juice behind all the action. The expense account crowd, the designated Washington power hitters were the ones who made the deals over three martini lunches. To be at that table, he knew he had to groom himself through innovation and insight towards the political side of the house.

He started playing golf at the best courses throughout Virginia even though he hated the game. He learned where the heavy hitters ate lunch and dinner and made sure he was occasionally seen in places like Charlie Palmer downtown, Old Ebbitt Grill, and Café Milano in Georgetown. You didn't just walk off the street into these places unless you had the juice or knew someone who did. He learned how to dress, filling his closet with tailored Hart, Shafter and Mark and Savoy Row suits.

By the time he was fifty, Crawford had run the table as far as a career in the Company went and was about to start a major effort for political office when Stone Gate had come along. He had been a hands down favorite in the Congressional back rooms where the real decisions are made and sailed through a closed session for directorship of the project. He had become the single point of contact for *all* Stone Gate operations with a limitless budget and the *off the chart* power to drop anyone into a hole if they meddled where they shouldn't be.
The FBI, the Attorneys General's office, and everybody else connected to DOJ stayed away from whatever Stone Gate was

involved with. Because of the untouchable aspect of the operation, the "Kingdom" title was now synonymous with the organization, the proverbial third rail in the ranks of the power brokers. You didn't touch it, and you damn sure didn't talk about it.

Clayton Edward Crawford was the man behind Stone Gate, and now Pryor was sitting in that man's office trying to think of how he was going to answer his question. *What were his expectations?*

"Ah, Sir, I am redoubling our efforts on the ground and I...."

"Why would you be redoubling your efforts if the first thing you did was incorrect?" interrupted Crawford. "How does that make sense?"

"Sir, I'm not sure what you want me to say."

Crawford smiled without humor. "Mike, do you know why it is so important we apprehend Agent Clark?"

"Because you gave an order. It's your directive," Pryor replied, growing increasingly uncomfortable with the conversation.

Crawford tapped the contents of his pipe into the large glass ashtray on his desk. "I need you to stop being a Colonel in the Marine Corps for just a minute, Mike."

"Sir?"

"Haven't you wondered *why* the directive was given?"

Pryor cleared his throat. "Sir, the *why* is above my pay grade. I.."

"You know I really do not like that phrase *"above my pay grade"*. You're not a mindless order taker, not some careerist Marine Colonel kissing the ass of every star that crosses your path. You're far beyond that, Mike."

"Yes, sir." More than anything, Pryor wanted to melt through the floor and get out of this office. Nothing good could come out of a prolonged conversation with the Director.

Crawford checked his watch and then looked up as if he had lost his train of thought. "The reason it's so important that Agent Clark be found and dealt with," he announced leaning back in his chair, "is that we now know that anyone who has direct contact with the Stone Gate anomaly as he did in Albuquerque is forever changed by the exposure no matter how brief. If the person somehow enters it again or comes in contact with it, catastrophic changes could happen."

"Sir? Changed how?"

"They are drawn to it. A connection is made on a level we do not understand yet. Agent Clark is headed this way. He cannot help himself."

"That's very interesting, Sir. Is there a change in your orders?"

Crawford thought for a moment. "I have a suspicion that Clark's trip to the Vatican may have something to do with the fact that he is so easily able to move around. He may have help."

"I'm not sure I'm following you, Sir. What kind of help?

"Do we know why Clark was at the Vatican in the first place?" asked Crawford, looking at his hands.

"Well, sir, according to reports and phone transcripts, he was summoned by Vatican officials because of his knowledge of the Stone Gate operation. They wanted information and they assumed he had it."

"Do you know what else was going on with Clark prior to his *Summons* to the Vatican?"

"Yes, Sir," replied Pryor. "He was involved in a stolen art case. I believe he picked up some religious artifacts in some town in Michigan."

Crawford nodded. "Do you know what those artifacts were?"

Pryor could see where this was headed. "I believe they were some sort of medals or Medallions. Sir, you don't think that these artifacts are somehow aiding Clark?"

Crawford let out a sigh as he stared at the ceiling. "Mike, if a year and a half ago, I had told you the United States Government had a device that allowed access to the space/time Continuum, a device that was invented by a retired aerospace engineer in a basement lab in Albuquerque, New Mexico, what would you have said?"

Pryor smiled. "I would have said it was impossible."

"Yes, I believe you would have said that, and you would have been wrong. We are now doing the impossible, Mike. It is also impossible for a man to get on a 747 in Sydney, Australia, fly 17 hours, and then leave that airplane without being seen by twenty highly trained agents. Do you see what I am getting at, Colonel?"
"Yes, sir. I think so."

"Listen, I know you are a very pragmatic person, someone who thoroughly assesses the facts before making a decision. It's one of the reasons you were recruited to work for this program. But, what I need from you now is to start embracing the impossible. Clark has some kind of help that we are not aware of, something that is allowing him to move undetected. I want you to find out what that is and stop him. He simply cannot be allowed anywhere near the anomaly. Things are far too precarious as it is. Am I making myself clear?"

"Yes, Sir." Pryor really had no idea what the Director was getting at...*magic medals? Super powers given to Clark by the Vatican? What the hell is he talking about?* Clark had simply been too quick. He must have exploited a gap in the surveillance ring. It had to be nothing more. To suggest otherwise was pure fantasy and an annoying waste of time.

"Start thinking outside the box on this, Mike. Find our missing FBI agent and get him in the ground. There is more at stake here than you know."

"Yes, Sir."

He sat, waiting for Crawford to say the meeting was over. Instead, the director punched in some numbers on his desk phone. "Yes, have the car ready. I need to be on the Hill in ten minutes." He hung up the phone and sat back in his chair, re-lighting his pipe. "Is there anything else?" he asked flatly.

"Ah, no, Sir. I have everything I need." He got out of his chair awkwardly and left the room, still not sure what the Director was driving at. As he stepped into the elevator outside the office, he knew he had to get more information about what really had gone on when Clark was at the Vatican.

The idea of magic medals playing any part in all this was a lot of nonsense in his mind, but on the other hand, the job he now held, protecting what he now protected, would have seemed like utter fiction a year ago. If Clark was indeed using some magical medallion or medals to move around, then everyone involved with Stone Gate was in a lot more trouble than any of them realized, a whole lot more. Things were getting more interesting by the minute.

Chapter Thirteen

The next morning, twenty eight hundred miles to the west at the Douglas Canadian border crossing, Clark sat in the grass on the wide-open slope watching the heavy traffic head through the gates. Peace Arch Park on the Canadian side was the only designated pedestrian walkway that crossed Interstate 5, which originated in San Diego and ended at the border where it turned into Highway 99. It would be an easy crossing with the city of Blaine, Washington, just on the other side.

The night before Clark had paid cash for his hotel room and had spent the time resting and hacking into Pell's computer and phone. He had been able to find power cords for both devices at Best Buy which was down just a block from the Super Eight Motel. Because Pell's computer had been set up with an XP operating system as most Government computers are, it was a relatively easy hack. Clark had been able to bypass the processing chip and gain entry to the menu. He was able to reboot in the "Safe" mode, giving him instant access to all of Pell's information.

The I-phone had been even easier. Pell's visible fingerprints were all over his computer screen, an easy target for latent prints. Clark had been careful to protect the prints until he got to a place where he had the time and privacy to lift them. During his active fieldwork with the FBI, he had attended many finger print identification and processing seminars along with Cyber Crime and computer classes. These were skills that were now serving him well. All he needed to lift the prints were a couple of number two pencils, some clear Scotch tape, and a bit of patience.

He had removed the Graphite lead from the pencils the night

before in his room. He ground it into a fine powder in one of the bathroom glasses and then sprinkled the fine dust on several of the prints on the computer screen. Gently, he had lifted three good prints from the monitor using the clear tape, hoping that one of the prints would unlock the finger print recognition device on the phone.

As he gently applied the first two prints to the device, the phone remained locked. But on the third, the familiar, multi-colored I-phone menu screen suddenly appeared. He was in. He was astounded by what he found on Pell's computer. He discovered file after file of operational information with numerous references to *"Stone Gate"* in particular and naming several senior individuals associated with the program.

Pell's direct handler was someone by the name of Mike Pryor. After cross-referencing the emails with the phone record, Clark was able to determine that Pryor was in Washington DC. With a few keystrokes he was able to identify Pryor's address or at least a location within several blocks of where the emails to Pell had originated.

The emails from Pryor were somewhat cryptic, carrying an edge of power seen when electronic commands came from a supervisor. They carried a passive aggressive mandate that left the receiver with little room for speculation. Pryor appeared to be somewhat of a hard ass, short in salutations, abrupt in his on-line communications with Pell. From his reading, it was obvious that Pell was an underling, someone who was trying to please his handlers at all cost. Over the course of his career, Clark had seen hundreds like him, fresh faced hard chargers right out of the Academy who desperately wanted to kick ass and take names, meat-eaters who carried their credentials and egos in the same place - right up front for the whole world to see. These were the kind of guys who loved *not* telling you they were in the FBI but "let it slip" when the badge was inadvertently exposed while paying for gas or a meal, or those who had had the *on-purpose* slip of the tongue in mixed company. Everybody wanted to be the cool guy. Problem is, you never knew who was really listening. Trying to impress people you didn't really know could get you killed. As far as Pell's phone and computer were concerned, Clark only needed a few minutes to get the information, knowing full well that both items would leave an electronic signature the moment they were activated. Only thing he needed now was a paper and pen. He had come full circle. It was the simple things that would get him where he needed to go.

Now, on the outside of it all looking in, he could see for the first time how disconnected he had grown over the years, how jaded he had become about life in general. Emotionally, the divorce had blown him out of the water. Everything had changed after Albuquerque. He could remember the day he woke up that early Monday morning and knew in his gut that the woman lying next to him no longer loved him. All the fires had gone out on both sides. They had drifted too far, becoming more like disinterested roommates than husband and wife.

There had been no arguing, no shouting over perceived wrongs and betrayals, just a slow steady death of real emotion and passion. It was actually a relief when the bureau told him he was being transferred to DC to work in the Art Crimes division. He had been relieved that he was leaving New Mexico and more importantly, Donna, his wife of sixteen years.

She was not going with him. She had had enough and said she would be just fine by herself. He had seen it coming but it still broke him in two when she said it out loud. Maybe that was the problem in a nutshell. They hadn't really talked about what had happened to him during those twenty-four days, locked up, re-programmed, and reeducated by the

Government. He had just taken the hit, crawled into an emotional corner, and let everything else burn down around him.

As he sat on the hillside watching the pedestrians walk through the Arch Bridge that led into Blaine, Washington, he wondered how Donna was doing now. Was she happy? Had she found what or maybe whom she needed in her life? He let the questions hang in the air, not willing to follow the reasoning, or even worse, the truth. He had let it happen, had been a willing participant in his own destruction.

Oddly, the delusion gave him comfort, thinking that she was still waiting for him back home; he was still holding on to the possibility that she recognized that she had made a mistake and wanted him back. The idea that she was happier with someone else was just too painful to think about. He would hang on to the fantasy. Besides, the clothes on his back and the fantasy of reconciliation were all he had left. Stone Gate had taken everything else.

An hour later and very much visible, he had crossed the border and was walking up to Mad Don Auto Mart in downtown Blaine, Washington. In the lot, five, ten, and fifteen-year-old cars sat side-by-side under brightly colored cardboard signs that said "Sweet" or "Low Mileage." It was the kind of place where a person could pay cash and drive off the lot without a lot of questions or heavy traceable paperwork. "Here's your money. Give me the keys. I'm out of here."

After looking a full ten minutes, Clark counted out seventy-three hundred dollars in cash and took the keys from the surprised salesmen. "You know, I think you're really gonna like this Malibu," he announced leaning into the driver's side window. Clark shook hands with the man and started the car. "Yeah, I think so too. Thank you."

"You know, you might want to think about our no-fault warranty. I think it's only about thirty dollars a month and it covers the power train, timing chain, and anythi…"

"No, thanks," interrupted Clark, dropping the car in gear. "I really need to be going."

"Oh, okay then, Mister Pell. I'll be sure and get that tag to your residence in a week or two."

Clark smiled and gave the man a thumbs-up and then drove out of the lot onto Peace Portal Avenue and headed south. As he moved through traffic, he smiled at how easy it had been to buy the car. The car had only cost fifty-eight hundred dollars. The rest of the seventy-five hundred had gone into the salesman's pocket, payment for discretion. Besides, it wasn't as if people were lining up to buy the faded blue 2005 Chevy Malibu, a car that could blend into the landscape yet was reliable enough to get him across country.

In the last three days he had read enough of Robashaw's diary to make him more than a little hesitant about using the flying Medallion. For now, driving to DC seemed to be the safest way to go. He had learned that Robashaw had spent three years stocking up supply caches all across the country. The stashes would make the trip across country halfway survivable. More importantly, travel would give him time to figure out why he was being pulled so hard. It would give him time to think.

Something out there was drawing him in, and that something knew who he was, knew what he was. He intuitively knew that when he finally arrived at the place he was drawn to, life as he now knew it would be over. *No, this is a one-way trip,* he thought, turning onto the freeway. He flicked on the radio and merged into the fast lane as the familiar intro of Green Day's song "American Idiot" came through. "Yeah," he said out loud, ..."*fitting*".

Chapter Fourteen

Hauser had been up since eight. After paying his room bill, he set out for the small corner café for breakfast. As he walked, he noticed patches of the snow that had fallen the night before in the building's shadows and the alleyways. It was cold outside, but the sun was shining, which lightened his mood considerably. He was amazed at how much better he felt than he did last night. He had slept soundly as his clothes dried by the heater. Putting on the dry clothing this morning was a comfort he hadn't experienced in days.

Stopping at the corner, he pushed open the heavy wood and glass door of the busy café as the inviting smell of fresh bread and coffee washed over him. Finding a vacant table towards the back of the room, he sat down and waited for the waitress. Scanning the crowd, he guessed that most of the men sitting at tables and standing at the counter were day laborers, the hard scrabble back bone that kept a city this size functioning. Carpenters, pipe fitters, bricklayers, and craftsmen filled the room, hard men who worked with their hands, men who took pride in what they did. They were the kind of people he had been raised around as a kid in Montana.

As he drank the strong black coffee that the waitress had just poured, he went over his options, possible courses of action that were growing fewer in number by the minute. His handlers would now know that something had gone wrong, that events of history had not changed. In his planning for the initial movement, a contingency of *"worst case"* scenarios had been established. If the time markers were missed and contact was lost, a second asset would be sent through the Continuum in hopes of providing a link up and possible safe return. The appearance zone would be the exact location as the first and at the same time plus 24 hours once contact had been lost.
Hauser checked his watch. In eleven and a half hours, a

second operator should be showing up in the park where he made his entry three days earlier. His role now would be to stay as unobtrusive as possible and be near the point of entry to await the next operator's arrival later that night. The next asset would be carrying instructions on whether the mission was still green or whether both were return. Either way it went, he would soon have an answer.

"What would you like?" questioned the heavyset waitress stepping up close to his table, the Northern Bavarian accent distinctive in her German.

Hauser smiled. "Ah, two eggs, toast, and bacon if you have it, please."

The woman wrote down the order and then gave him a disapproving look. "I haven't seen you in here before. Are you new to the area?"

"Yes, yes, I am. Just following the work."

The woman put her hands on her hips. "I know all the mugs that come into my place. They all look the same to me. You look different. What work do you do?" It was an impertinent question, but one he could not ignore.

He could feel the sweat run down his back. He needed to be very careful; this could get dicey. "I'm a pipefitter," he replied, hoping the lie would hold.

The woman laughed a snorting reply, "A pipefitter with those hands? My third husband was a pipefitter, had the hands of a gorilla. You have the hands of an accountant. I don't think you're being truthful."

Hauser had no idea what to do next. He wasn't sure if he was actually being challenged by the woman about his profession or if she was just busting his balls. Whatever she was doing, several other men seated nearby were starting to take notice of their conversation. Thinking fast, he leaned closer to the woman and smiled. "Well, my dear, I didn't say I was a very good pipefitter," he said softly with a wink.

The woman suddenly laughed and tapped him on the shoulder. "Fair enough," she said walking away. "Nice to be around honesty, unlike most of these sods." Several of the men laughed as she moved her great girth between the tables on her way to the kitchen. Evidently she was the owner and something of an institution among the regulars. More importantly, she had given Hauser a tacit level of approval. Right now, he would take all the luck he could get.

****

In the two years since he had first met Clayton Crawford, this was only the third time they had physically been in the same room.

"Sir, as you know, we have missed our time line marker with the asset. We are now within the twenty four hour window for the second jump," announced Shaw, handing the mission file across the desk.

The Director had arrived at Shaw's office just before nine that morning, his presence sucking all the oxygen out of the room. In that respect Shaw could not remember a time when he had been this nervous giving a briefing.

Crawford took the file. "What are our expectations?" he asked studying the data.

"Sir, as you are aware, the target is fluid. The venue that was chosen for the contact brought the target within acceptable range. The planning that went into this access was very detailed. We are currently working on another plan that would put a second asset close to the target."

Crawford closed the file and laid it on the desk. "Okay," he replied with a sigh. "I have had probably thirty recent meetings with physiologists, population migratory experts, sociologists and countless other experts in the fields of physics, religion, and social consciousness. We now have a pretty good idea of what will happen to this planet if we are successful in our endeavors. My question to you, Doctor Shaw, is do we have better than an even chance of our asset actually getting close enough to kill Adolf Hitler in 1939?"

That was exactly the kind of question Shaw had been worried about since the Nazi had suddenly appeared in the jump station. A wild card of fate that had been dropped on the table, his presence had changed the game. Men like Crawford dealt in absolutes, black and white, efforts that could be measured and acted upon, usually with a set of hard and fast rules that followed most scientific problems and their subsequent solutions.

But in this case, the rules for the entire Stone Gate project were being written by the minute. There was no long term statistical data to draw from, no proven analytics to base a theory on or even a confirmed viable course of action to take if something like this happened. Every time they had sent someone through the Continuum, they had learned something new. And to the great frustration of those running the project, the results were never the same.

What Shaw had learned from his time on the project was that the Continuum was not like a brick and mortar doorway that would stay in a fixed solid location, but a passageway that was almost fluid, easily affected by external and internal energy and, to some extent, the human beings being sent through it. In science the "human factor" always produced a high level of uncertainty when working towards predicted results. Stone Gate, with all its mind-bending power, was the mother of unpredictability.

"Sir, I can tell you with some degree of certainty that we can send one of our assets back to 1939." Shaw continued, "With some planning we can probably get him within sight of Hitler. But what that asset actually does once he has the opportunity to make the shot is still the open question in my mind."

Crawford thought for a moment. "Do you think we are sending the wrong people in to do the task?"

Shaw knew he had to be careful here, knowing full well that expressing verbal doubt about the project could be lethal. "No, sir, I don't. But I do have a theory, something that might explain a few things."

Crawford sat back in his chair smiling slightly. "Go ahead, Doctor. I would like to hear your theory."

Shaw cleared his throat nervously. "Well, I know that the project has had some success in altering recorded history. We stopped the '87-flu epidemic that killed almost a million people, and we stopped the assassination of President Obama last year. Both of these events were major in their own right but small in the cosmic scale of things."

"Go on," replied Crawford lighting his pipe.

"Well, sir, I don't want to sound pejorative here, but those operations were minor league ball compared to this. As to the question concerning whether the right people are being sent to do the task, we trained, prepared and equipped a very experienced Navy SEAL, a man with extensive special operations experience in combat zones. Yet he has failed the mission. Why?"

"Okay, I'm listening. Why did our asset fail?"

"Sir, maybe, just maybe, there is a measurable tolerance of cosmic and social change that is allowed in our three dimensional reality. It's possible that World War Two was *supposed* to happen and that Adolf Hitler was the designated catalyst for the current progression of events. It's possible that something on the emotional level of World War Two cannot be reversed or stopped. Maybe we are dealing with a Higher Power, a solid universal law we are not familiar with."

"So, Doctor Shaw, you're saying that *fate* or God or some other ascension force intervened and stopped our highly trained assassin? I didn't know you were religiously bent. In my experience the answers that religion tends to provide are an over simplification of a complex reality."

Shaw took a deep breath, knowing that he had already said too much. "Sir, what I am saying is that it was nearly impossible for him *not* to succeed. It should have happened, but it didn't. I am beginning to think we are getting into new territory here as it pertains to cosmic cause and effect."

Crawford thought for a moment and then stood up, tapping his pipe out in the ashtray on Shaw's desk. "I see where your theory is going, Doctor Shaw. I appreciate your efforts in trying to quantify why certain things happen. But a decision has been made in this matter, and what I need from you now is your dedication and leadership in seeing that this mission is a success. A great crime against humanity has been committed, a crime we now have the ability to erase from history." He pushed the file across the desk. "Send in the second asset, Doctor. It's time to change the world."

Chapter Fifteen

Clark had been heading east on I-94 out of Spokane for several hours and was starting to see restaurant and other Idaho business signs and advertisements. As the miles rolled by, he had begun to feel the need to make bold moves soon if he was to have any chance of making it to DC alive. Odds were that the Kingdom had picked up his trail at the border. He knew that his continued freedom was now measured in hours at most.

Seeing a wide-open expanse followed by the exit sign for Moscow, Idaho, he decided that this was as good a place as any to put his plan in motion. The openness free of innocent bystanders and witnesses would work in his favor. *Yeah, northern Idaho would work,* he told himself pulling into the Shell Station. He turned off the car and sat thinking over how he was going to start. Across from the station past a three-strand barbed wire fence on the other side of the road was an expansive soybean field, a perfect place to learn how to fly.

He opened the backpack and pulled out Robashaw's faded blue leather diary. Thumbing through the worn pages, he found the dog-eared entry the old man had written about how he had first learned of the Gold Medal's power. "Amazing" didn't come close to describing the man's entry.

August 17, 2012

This morning I put the gold medal around my neck and immediately felt it press itself onto my chest. It is a strange feeling but not at all uncomfortable. I started walking down the driveway towards Tomlinson road. After awhile I felt the need to run, something I have not felt compelled to do in over twenty years to say the least. Feeling a bit foolish, I began to trot, hoping none of my neighbors would drive by and catch this sixty-year-old man with bad knees trying to run. Feeling quite proud of myself as I picked up speed, I got cocky and increased my stride. That is when I stumbled and things got crazy. I fell forwards, arms out stretched, but instead of falling on my face, I stayed horizontal four feet off the ground, cleared the end of the driveway, the road, and the barbed wire fence on the other side. By a conservative estimate I flew a good fifty yards before rolling into the weeds in Mason's pasture. The cows were very interested.

My God, what have I discovered?

"Jesus," whispered Clark out-loud, looking up from the diary. Was he actually going to bet his life on this? Is this what things had come to? Everything he had just read went against all logic, all common sense. He knew that people could not fly, yet he had seen the Silver Medal's power first hand and felt that mind-blowing effect. Looking at the Gold Medallion, he knew in his heart that whatever power the Medals had did not come from this reality. The Medallions had not been brought into this world for cheap tricks and parlor games, and he knew instinctively that it had to be for a higher calling, some noble cause of staggering significance. As he looked at the magnificent medals in the light of the bright sun, he could not shake the notion that somehow they were connected to the spiritual side of life, objects that had been used to change the world. He was sure that they were that important...that "*sacred,*" he whispered.

****

It was just after eleven o'clock that same morning when Mike Pryor's cell phone rang. He had been in the office all morning reading the SITREPS from the field, growing more agitated by the hour at the lack of information concerning Agent Clark's whereabouts. He looked at the number of the incoming call, stunned. It was Pell, the same agent who had been found dead in the trunk of his rental car on the island of Tonga just a week ago.

"Who is this?" he demanded answering the call.

"You must be Mike Pryor," replied Clark cheerfully, turning on the car air conditioner. "I guess you know who this is?"

"Agent Clark? You got brass balls using the phone of the Federal Agent you killed. Whatever edge you thought you had, you just threw away, pal."

Clark laughed. "Listen up, dip-shit. I am calling you so we can make a deal, a good one."

"A deal? You gotta be shitting me! The only deal you're going to get from me is a bullet through the brain and a really deep grave. I don't need to hear a goddamn thing you have to say, Clark. Oh, and just so you know, I'll be able to track your cell phone in about ah, let's see, twenty-three seconds. No, make that fifteen. You just committed suicide, dumbass."

"Okay, you feel better now that you've given me your tough guy speech? Listen up, Pryor. I have something in my possession that is a game changer. Your superiors are definitely going to want it. I know all about Stone Gate, and in exchange I want a one-way ticket in your magic machine to a time and location of my choice. I promise that what I have will be more than a fair trade."

Clark could tell by the long pause on the phone that he had struck a very sensitive nerve. "I have no idea what you're talking about, Clark," replied Pryor. "Tell you what though, you just stay right where you are and some of my guys will be right there. This will be over very soon."

"Kind of figured you'd say that. I guessed that I would have to show just how valuable my bargaining chips really are. It's gonna make this a really unfair fight though. Anyway, we'll be talking soon, Pryor. If you're smart, you'll make a deal. Talk to you later, dick head." He disconnected the call, pulled out the battery and tossed the phone into the back seat. He had Pryor's phone number memorized and all the rest of the numbers written down. He'd use disposable phones from now on. There was no use making it too easy for his pursuers.

Clark was starting to get past the emotional and reactionary aspect of his plan and into the real work and thought of controlling the "battle space," as it were. Simply running was not going to make it; the Kingdom had more assets, better and faster movement capability, and total autonomy as it related to direct action. Playing by their rules, linear warfare, would get him killed in hours. The Kingdom's weakness was the centralized command and control structure. Only one, maybe two, were calling all the shots for the entire Stone Gate operation.

This old, iron-fisted style of control that most government bureaucracies used even to this day had a weakness. Because all operational decisions were made by senior management, little ownership was taken in solving problems at the street level. The need for permission and approval to address crises in the field created delays of action, much like those suffered in his own FBI. The ability of the Kingdom to respond to a major wild card factor, ie someone with a Medallion that allowed them to fly or become invisible, would be poor. You couldn't conduct surveillance on what you couldn't see. You couldn't follow a suspect with conventional helicopters, cars, and planes if the suspect himself was flying. These were all major vulnerabilities he intended to exploit.

Clark had studied Robashaw's cache map. He knew food and other supplies had been stashed clear across country. He understood Robashaw's flight patterns and knew the cache locations. If he conducted his travel under the cover of darkness, he would be nearly impossible to track. Robashaw had been on the run and survived for three years using the medals. It wouldn't take him three years to get to DC. Now all he had to do was put the medals to the test and learn to fly.

Confident he was taking the right course of action, he picked up his backpack, locked the keys in the car, and trotted across the highway. He guessed that he would probably have less than an hour before Pryor's people started showing up. He was cutting it close for getting the use of the Gold Medallion down and, depending on how steep the learning curve was, maybe too close.

With excitement building, he ducked under the top strand of the barbed wire fence and walked into the field. Draping the Gold Medallion around his neck, he immediately felt it suck down over his heart. If this didn't work, Pryor was right, this would all be over real soon. Looking up into the bright early morning sun, he zipped up his jacket, tightened the shoulder straps on his backpack, and took a deep breath.

He had no idea what to expect as he began to trot through the knee-high grass. His last thought, just before he broke into a dead run, was how ridiculous he would look to anyone passing by. With arms and legs pumping, he sprinted four more steps, and then, with total abandon, leapt, arms stretched in front of him as if he were diving into a pool.

As if in a fantastic mind-bending dream, he skimmed across the field, four feet off the ground, a solid seventy yards before tumbling into the damp sod. Astonished and relieved beyond reason at what had just happened, he lay on his back, arms out-stretched, laughing, and looking up into the clear blue Idaho sky. He caught his breath, sat up, looked around, and then shouted at the top of his lungs, "Holy shit!"

****

Hauser stood under the orange glow of the streetlight just before midnight watching a light snow silently fall. From where he stood, he could see the area where he had made his own landing several days earlier. If all went according to plan, in exactly four minutes and thirty seconds, a second team member would step through the Continuum, bringing welcome news on the next phase of the operation. The night had grown cold sending most of the restaurant and shop pedestrians indoors. Relieved, he could see that he was the only person in the area as he looked around. Several cars and heavy trucks rumbled by on the slushy streets but not near the same traffic volume he had noted during the day. People were in bed under dry roofs oblivious to the pending drama in the small dimly lit park.

Hauser checked his watch. "Thirty seconds," he whispered pulling his collar tight. *Damn, it's getting cold,* he thought stamping his feet. Just as he was sure that whatever happened in the next twenty seconds would not be seen, he caught movement off to his right.

"Son of a bitch," he whispered as a German police officer on foot patrol came into view. Reaching deep in his coat pocket, he gripped his pistol, already dreading the course of action he was being forced to take. Hauser watched him come closer. *He is just some guy trying to get through his shift,* he thought, thumbing the weapon off "safe". *Jesus, why now? Why did he have to walk by the only spot in this whole goddamned city where he didn't need to be?*

Killing a monster is one thing, but killing some working stiff who just happens to be in the wrong place at the wrong time, is off the charts bad Karma. The cop is about to die and will never know the reason why. Hauser checked his watch and silently counted down... Five, four, three, two, one. The officer was now twenty feet away and still walking in his direction when suddenly a blinding blue-white flash of light split the darkness in all directions, followed by a tremendous wind-rushing sound. As cold as it was already, the temperature seemed to drop ten more degrees.

Hauser closed the gap to the stunned cop in two strides and knocked the man off his feet with a flying elbow to the right side of his face. In all his time with the teams in all the missions, Hauser had never killed an innocent civilian, and he was damn sure not going to start now. The officer slammed onto the sidewalk in a heap, knocked unconscious by the vicious hit. Hauser looked to the landing area and spotted the dark shape, the man lying on his back in the snow.

Recognizing that he had little to no time, he grabbed the officer's arm and quickly dragged him out of the glow of the street lights and into the bushes near the welcome team member who was now on his knees vomiting loudly.

Chapter Sixteen

The Bell Ranger came in low from the west following the highway from Seattle all the way to the Idaho border. In a fit of fury, Pryor had notified Agent Frost and his team that he had just received a phone call from Clark and that he wanted the FBI Agent's 'head on a stick within the hour.' Frost had never seen nor heard the Deputy Director so worked up before. Whatever Clark had said had really spun him up good. From the copilot's seat, Frost pointed to the large open parking lot on the backside of the Shell Station. "Put us down there," he commanded.

Frost and two agents quickly stepped out of the Ranger and headed across the parking lot after landing. "Check with the attendant. See if anyone has seen our guy," announced Frost to the other men. "There's a car back here I want to check out."

Clark had watched the chopper land while lying in three-foot-high weeds a quarter mile up the hill. To calm his nerves and ready his next move, he slowly got to his knees. He watched the men as they walked around his car and the surrounding area, weapons at the ready. Suddenly jolted from his perception of safety, he watched as the station attendant pointed in his direction while talking to one of his pursuers. "Shit," he whispered ducking down. He had to move now. He was well within rifle range and the helicopter could be on him in minutes. Scrambling to his feet, he started running farther up the slope; if they were going to catch him they would have to work for it.

"Sir!" shouted one of the men. "I've got movement... three o'clock at about four hundred yards!"
"If you have a shot, take it!" shouted Frost, running back to

the chopper that was beginning to spin up.

As he stumbled and ran farther up the slope, Clark felt two rounds from a heavy caliber rifle zip by. *It is now or never*, he thought sprinting as fast as he could. *Hopefully I have enough speed.* With three bounding steps he leapt forward with arms out-stretched.

Back on the highway, the agent firing the PSG-1 looked over the top of his scope in stunned amazement. The man he had been aiming at had suddenly left the ground in a slow high arc and was now only a small black dot just about to clear the top of the ridge. He shook his head still not believing what he was seeing. The man was flying, honest to God, no shit... flying!

"Get on the bird!" he heard Frost shout through his earpiece. Still stunned by what he had witnessed, the agent ran back to the helicopter and jumped into the back seat as it lifted off.

"Sir, did you see what I saw?" shouted the agent grabbing his headset and buckling his seat belt.

"Yeah, you said you had movement," replied Frost from the front seat. "Did you hit him?"

The agent shook his head. "No, Sir, he just flew away."

"He did what?"

"One second he was there running, and the next moment he was off the ground and flying."

Frost turned in his seat. "If you missed the shot, you can tell me, okay? I do know that SEALS sometimes miss."
"Sir, I'm telling you that the guy left the ground and flew off. I still cannot believe what I saw."

Frost turned to the pilot. "Did you see anything like that?"

"No, Sir, nothing like that. We should be on top of the area about now."

In all his forty-three years, Clark had never felt this kind of exhilaration, this much mind-blowing freedom and excitement. With arms outstretched and legs stiff, he cleared the top of the ridge by twenty feet, the brown rocky ground flashing by in a blur. Over the top he flew, dropping down the backside of the hill, barely skimming the treetops. His speed was now tearing tears from his eyes, making it hard to see. He made a mental note about getting goggles as the wind roared by his ears.

A hundred yards behind, the Bell Ranger banked a hard right and then started climbing towards the top of the ridge. "I don't see any sign of him," announced the pilot checking his air speed indicator.

"Circle back around," commanded Frost scanning the ground below. "I want to be sure he isn't lying down in that tall grass."

Clark had no idea how fast he was skimming over the treetops, the familiar smell of mountain pine heavy in the air. He soon discovered that if he bent his knees, his speed decreased. If he panned his hands right or left, he turned in that direction. The physical sensation of unrestricted flight was the most incredible feeling he had ever had. It made him giddy with joy. His only trepidation now was that he had no real sense of direction. From this height and speed, the ground was nothing more than a blurred green carpet. He would have to slow down or get higher in order to see and aim for any prominent terrain feature. For all he knew, with all his turning in wide sweeping arcs, he could be heading back in the direction of his pursuers.

Deciding that he had to get his bearings, he lowered his arms to his side, pulled his knees into a tight tucked position, and quickly dropped from the sky - in fact, a little too quickly. The trees suddenly rose up from the ground at an alarming rate. He was falling too fast, and before he could recover, he crashed through the limbs and leaves, thudding to the hard ground. Dazed, he rolled onto his back with a grunt, trying to catch the breath that had been knocked out of his lungs. "Jesus Christ, " he moaned rolling onto his side. *Take offs are a breeze,* he thought, slowly sitting up, pulling small twigs from his hair. *Landings are a bitch.* He knew he could not take too many falls like this in the future without risking serious injury. This time he had been lucky.

Still in pain from the fall, he was getting to his feet just as the Bell Ranger flashed by overhead. Judging by the sound of the engine, they were not slowing down. Evidently they hadn't seen his fall and thought they were still in hot pursuit. He knew that if he was going to get any kind of closure on this he would have to let them know just how powerful his weapons really were. He would give them a demonstration, show them what they were up against. As he took a couple of quick steps, he left the ground, hoping the men in the helicopter would be just as in awe of what he was about to do as he was. Everything depended on it.

****

Shivering more from adrenalin than the cold, Hauser quickly stepped up to the man who was slowly getting to his feet and still trying to catch his breath. "Hey, brother, you okay?" announced Hauser holding the man's elbow.
"Yeah, yeah, I, ah, think I'm okay. Shit, is it always like that? Feels like I just got shot out of a canon. Son of a bitch." He bent down, holding his knees and wretched. "Ahh, God, that's rough," he said, wiping his mouth.

In the dim light, Hauser could see that the man was close to his own age and carried the unmistakable, hard to define, physical presence of an operator. The way he spit and then pinched off one nostril clearing his nasal passages pointed to a man who had lived down range for some time, having long since stopped trying to impress anyone with personal hygiene protocol.

"You Hauser?" he asked in perfect German, wiping his nose.

"Yep, and you?"

"My name is Campbell, John Campbell, Sargent Major, US Army, CAG. "

Hauser shook hands. "Gotta tell you, John, it's great to see you."

Campbell smiled while looking up into the night sky. "Well kind of a mixed blessing for me, pard. On one hand I am getting the chance to do something that only a handful of people in all the world have ever done. For that I am grateful. On the other hand I would not even be here if you had succeeded in your mission, which means we are now probably in a pretty tough spot."

Hauser nodded. "You're right. I fucked up. I choked, and I am man enough to admit that. Let's get under cover somewhere, and I will fill you in."

Campbell thought for a moment. "All right. Sounds good. I am about to freeze to death. You know a place to go?"
"Yeah, there's an inn about a block away. It's warm and dry, a good place to figure things out."

"Lead the way," replied Campbell stamping his feet. "Jesus, it's cold out here."

Hauser nodded, motioning to the unconscious German police officer lying half under the snow-crusted bushes a few feet away. "We've gotta take care of him first."

"Who's that?" questioned Campbell suddenly alarmed.

"It's a German police officer. He saw you flash in. I had to clip him."

"Holy shit, is he dead?"

Hauser walked over and knelt down beside the officer. He pulled off his glove with his teeth so he could check for his pulse. "Not yet, but he will be." He rolled the man on his stomach and in one swift motion cradled the man's head in his arms and snapped back his chin, breaking the man's upper vertebrae with an audible, sickening snap, a move he had been taught a hundred years ago.

"Jesus," whispered Campbell looking down the empty street and then back at the two. In his Special Operations career he had taken countless lives, seen hundreds die, but watching the SEAL kill the man like that was like watching an animal being slaughtered. It was brutal, almost clinical ....deeply disturbing.

"Help me drag him onto the sidewalk," commanded Hauser stuffing his gloves in his coat pocket and grabbing the now lifeless officer's arm. "This has to look like he slipped on the ice and broke his neck. Here grab the other arm." As the snow began to fall harder, they carefully placed the officer on his back on the icy sidewalk, his arms out stretched like a macabre snow angel.

As they quickly walked away, Hauser worked to justify the murder in his mind. He had killed an innocent man, someone who had nothing to do with the mission, someone with a family, maybe a wife and children, people who cared about him, people who would be looking for his return. The only way he kept himself from total debilitating despair was to stay focused on the mission. Collateral damage was always a bitch and always a heart breaker. He had seen this before in Africa on a mission when indirect fire had been called in on a small village as they were being extracted during an operation that had gone bad from day one. Twenty-eight people had died that afternoon, their only crime - being in the right spot at the wrong time. A coordinates miscalculation had brought down steel rain, and there had been nothing anyone could do about it, nothing. No one had said a word over the intercom as the extraction bird had done a slow pass over the still smoking compound. The hard reality of the dark side of war had lain scattered about the red clay clearing like broken dolls in the rain. Some things were just too raw to talk about.

Shoving his hands deep in his coat pockets, Campbell snorted and spit, still trying to clear his sinuses. "I think that guy probably deserved better than that," he announced softly, the snowflakes settling on his eyelashes. "No telling what future events his dying might affect."

Hauser suddenly stopped. "Hey listen, Campbell, you got something to say, you'd better get it off your chest right now. You read me, pal?"

Campbell spit again and then stepped up within inches of Hauser's nose. "Yeah, I got something to say, *pal*. Because of your fuck-up, I am here, sent to un-fuck-up whatever you did. This is turning into mission failure check mark real quick, and that is unacceptable in my book."

"Is that right?"

"That's right there, hot shot. We were told to have zero

contact with the locals, or were you out doing pushups the day that bit of information was disseminated."

"Fuck you, Campbell. This is my op and...."

"Not any more, Chief," interrupted Campbell. "You've been demoted. The only reason I have not capped your ass like I was instructed to if I ever met you was that I was just so surprised you were still alive."

"Well, I'm right here, tough guy. Carry out your goddamned orders."

Campbell leveled a steely gaze, his voice barely a whisper. "You feel that, Hauser, that hard object against your goddamned gut? That's my suppressed 40-caliber. It's got a four-pound trigger pull and it's cocked. Now you want to start playing by my rules, or do I dump you right here, right now? Your choice, Chief."

Hauser held the man's gaze, knowing in his heart that if the tables were turned he would be saying and doing the same thing. He stepped back while blowing a frosted breath into the night sky. "All right, okay, I was out of line. Where do we go from here?"

Campbell smiled. "You know, I really think we need to do this thing together. Just check with me before you kill anyone else, okay? I got German relatives around here somewhere. I would hate to get vaporized because you croked some Kraut."
"What about your orders?" questioned Hauser, smiling.

Campbell took his hands out of his pockets and cupped his hands, blowing on his fingers. "Fuck those guys. If they want you dead, then they can do it themselves when we get back."

Hauser pointed down the street. "You really think we're gonna pull this off?"

Campbell laughed and stared walking.   "Hell no, we're fucked big time.   I just wanted to give you some encouragement. Nothing worse than a SEAL pissing himself."

Hauser looked up into the snow-filled gloom and laughed. Yeah, Campbell was right. There was nothing worse.

Chapter Seventeen

From his hiding position under the trees, Clark watched as the chopper slowed and then settled into a wide low arc above the ridge. For Clark the sensation of being hunted was one of both giddy exhilaration and nearly overpowering dread, knowing full well that if spotted the designated marksman on the bird would drop him in an instant. He knew that he would not miss a second time.

The helicopter appeared to be staying at an altitude of about eight hundred to a thousand feet, a height he could easily reach in seconds. His primary concern before breaking cover and running down the slope to take off in flight was avoiding flying into the rotor or tail rotor when making his approach.

****

"Sir, I think we lost him," announced the pilot over the radio. "He's undercover somewhere."

"Take another pass on the west side of the ridge," replied Frost as he scanned the ground with his binoculars. "I know that son of a bitch is close. I can feel it."

"Yes, sir." Suddenly the pilot jerked back in his seat as if he had been shot. "Jesus!" he shouted over the radio. "Look at that!"

Frost turned to the front and was stunned to see the soles of Clark's shoes as he flew unassisted thirty yards directly in front of the chopper. The man was actually flying, the wind ripping at his clothes.

"You see this, right?" questioned the pilot quickly raising the dark helmet visor.

Frost shook his head…"Unbelievable," he whispered, still not comprehending what he was looking at.

"Sir, what do you want me to do?" questioned the pilot, his voice cracking with fear. The sight of a man in clear unassisted flight was both wonderful and terrifying at the same time.

"Can you get a shot?" shouted Frost.

"Sir?" replied the sniper, mesmerized by what he was seeing.

"I said, can you get a shot?"

"Sir, we are looking at a guy who is flying for God's sake - flying. And you want me to shoot him down? Shit, if this guy can fly there's no telling what else he can do. If you really want him shot, sir, then you're going to have to do it."

"So you are disobeying my direct order? Is that the case here?" replied Frost turning in his seat.

"That's right, sir. You want to bring down the flying man, then you're going to have to do it."

"I'm with him on that, Agent Frost," announced the pilot. "This is way over our pay grade."

Shaking his head in a mixture of awe and frustration, Frost watched as Clark continued to fly ahead of the chopper. "Sir, we are also getting low on fuel," announced the pilot. "We are going to have to do something here fairly quickly."

"You're shitting me, right?" replied Frost angrily. "We cannot lose this guy."
"Sir, I cannot argue with what the fuel gauge tells me. We are going to have to refuel and pretty soon."

Before Frost could answer, Clark suddenly banked a hard left and dropped from view. "Jesus, did you see that?" shouted the pilot twisting in his seat. "He's headed down. Unbelievable!"

"Follow him," Frost directed, tightening his lap belt. "Stay on him the best you can."

The sniper could be heard chuckling over the radio. "Holy shit!"

To Clark, the sensation of flying was close to the experience of skydiving. The sensation of wind flowing past his ears, the pressure of the wind against the legs and arms were the same. The only major difference - he had complete control over his altitude gain and descent. As he dropped from the sky, he now knew that no modern aircraft would be able to match his ability to maneuver. He could turn sharper, drop faster, and rise more quickly than any fixed wing or rotor aircraft he knew of. He would be able to outfly them all. That realization gave him an immense sense of power.

Suddenly getting ground rush, he quickly stretched out of his tight tuck, pulled his knees up, and took a nearly vertical seated position twenty feet off the ground, gently sinking through the trees onto the rocky ridge below. Seconds later the chopper roared over the treetops in hot pursuit. Taking a knee under the bows of a towering pine, Clark took the Gold Medal off his neck and slipped the Silver Medal on, immediately feeling the heavy medallion suck back onto his chest. "Now it gets fun," he whispered out loud.

The chopper was now landing in a small clearing a hundred yards farther up the ridge. Clark took a deep breath and stepped out from under the tree. For several minutes he watched as two men armed with long guns, jumped from the chopper and began to move in his direction. He knew that there was no way he would not be seen yet the men, now thirty yards away and closing, were oblivious to his presence. They were close enough now that he could hear their labored breathing as they ran in the higher altitude. He watched as they trotted by, passing him by inches. Holy shit, he almost said out loud.

He watched as the sniper knelt down and scanned the woods below the ridge through his scope. "Nothing moving down there."

Frost lifted his binoculars and scanned the tree line. "There's no way a man can move that fast through the woods. It just is not possible. We saw him go down right here."

The pilot's voice came through Frost's earpiece. "Sir, I am about to red line on fuel. What are your instructions?"

Frost thought for a moment. "All right, pull the ruck sacks out of the back and leave them there. Head back and get fuel. We still have a good six hours of daylight left. We'll be checking the area. Pick us up here when you're done. Mark our coordinates."

"Roger that."

Frost watched the pilot unload his backpack and the snipers ruck through his binoculars. "Let's go get our gear and check this whole ridgeline. The son of a bitch has got to be here."

***

He had had to move at a full sprint over the rocky ground to get to the chopper and now stood by as the pilot opened the back door. His plan had been to quickly change the medals and fly off in a different direction, but when he saw the pilot opening the doors and unloading gear, he could not pass on the opportunity. As the pilot closed the rear door on the left side, Clark slid into the back seat from the right. The pilot came around to close and lock the door, sealing in the invisible passenger. Within minutes they were airborne and skimming the tree tops on their way back to Spokane.

Clark sat back in the soft leather seat thinking that he could get used to this kind of control, this power. He could go anywhere. He could see things that he would otherwise not be allowed to see and hear things not meant to be heard. He knew that in the wrong hands, the power of the Medals could be used for ill intent. A sudden jolt of clarity washed over him at the realization that he was now using the Medals, using their power to shape events and was losing a sense of respect for their power. The Medallions were not of this world and surely not designed for subversion. But then again, maybe the true purpose of the Medals had been to promote an idea, to solidify a point of view, in this case - a view, a movement so strong that the world had been changed forever.... maybe.

Chapter Eighteen

Mike Pryor had been receiving nearly hourly situational reports from field agents all morning. They were evidently close to catching Clark in Idaho. After he had been spotted, an intense ground search had begun with additional assets brought into the area to assist Frost. Hopefully it was only a matter of time until Clark was in a body bag.

Pryor had just finished a terse phone conversation with Crawford that dispelled any ambiguity concerning what should be done with Agent Clark. He locked his desk and was preparing to leave to meet his wife downtown for lunch when his cell phone rang. "Pryor."

"Hey, tough guy. It's your ole buddy - Clark. Just wanted to check in and thank you for that chopper ride back to Spokane."

Pryor could feel the blood drain from his head as he slowly sat back down behind his desk.

"Yo, Mike, you there?"

"Yeah, I'm here. It's just strange talking to a dead man, Clark."

"Wow, Mike, that's it? That's the best comeback you have? Gosh, I'm all a quiver. Listen, dick-head, I am trying to save your life here, okay? I really am."

"You do know, Clark, your location is being traced. You're not hiding very well. You must have a death wish."

"Yeah, I know all about that secret squirrel computer you

have in the basement that pinpoints cell phone calls. Tell you what, pard, I will make it easy for you. I'll tell you where I am right now. Are you ready? I am standing on the corner of Elm and Hasting streets in downtown Spokane, just about four miles from where I got off of one of your really nice helicopters. Now, how's that for being helpful?"

"Just stay right there, hero, and some of my people will be right there to help you out."

"No can do, buddy. I am just doing this little cat and mouse game to show you that I cannot be caught and to give you an idea just how formidable an enemy I can be."

"Really?"

"Yeah, really, Mike. You see I know you did not even bother to pass my offer up the food chain. You didn't relate the fact that I am willing to make a deal with you people."

"And why would I do that? What could you possibly do other than be a minor pain in my ass, a pain with a very short life span, I might add. I don't believe in the Easter Bunny, Big Foot, or Global Warming and I sure as hell don't believe in Magic Medals. You're a dead man, Clark. That I believe in."

"Jesus, there you go with the threats. Not impressed, Mike. So here is what I am going to do. I am going to keep making you look bad to your superiors until they get the messages that you're either incompetent or that you're in on it - my continued survival. Anyway you slice it, Mike ole buddy, you come out on the short end. Meanwhile, as I stay just out of your reach, I start leaking big time to the press some of that really dark stuff you folks are into. What do you think, Mike? Do I have your attention now?"

"Well, this has been a great conversation, Clark. But I think your time is up. A BOLO has been put out on you with every state and federal agency in the country. In fact, a unit should be at your location…. let's see… probably about now."

"Yeah, I see them," replied Clark calmly, keeping his back pressed firmly against the brick wall of the Starbucks coffee shop. He pushed the disconnect button on the disposable phone that he had picked up earlier that afternoon at Wal-Mart and watched as two more marked Spokane Police Department units slid to a stop in front of the coffee shop. Minutes later a third dark colored sedan pulled up with several plainclothes individuals inside. Clark stood a mere feet away from his pursuers, invisible, still wearing the Silver medal around his neck. He was amazed at how much fun it was to stand practically in the middle of all this law enforcement activity, knowing that all their efforts were for him.

"Sir, he is not here," one of the plainclothes agents spoke into his phone as he walked back to his car. "There is nothing here."

"Goddamnit!" shouted Pryor. "He said he saw you. I was just talking to the son of a bitch three minutes ago."

"Sorry, sir. There is nobody here."

Pryor slammed the office door shut, realizing that maybe he had underestimated just how resourceful Clark really was. "He is there!" he shouted. "You're missing something."

As the street began to clear, Clark stepped out from the side of the building and quickly crossed the road. Smiling, he re-dialed Pryor's number. "Hey, dick head. That response time was outstanding. Hell, those guys really look sharp. You want me to describe what your folks were wearing?"
Pryor gripped the phone, his knuckles white with rage. "What do you want, Clark."

"Okay, good, Mike. Do I have your attention now?"

"You have my attention. What do you want?" he asked, sitting down behind his desk.

"All right, pard. Here we go. Make sure you write this down, Mike. I don't want you to forget anything. I know how much you upper echelon guys have to deal…"

"Just get on with it, you son of a bitch," Pryor interrupted, trying to maintain his composure. "What do you want?"

Clark laughed as he continued down the sidewalk, being careful to keep his voice down as he passed several people walking by. There was no use shaking up the locals with invisible voices.

"Okay, Mike, here we go, one more time. What I want is a free trip in that magic machine of yours."

"Don't know what you're talking about, but go on," replied Pryor doing everything he could to keep from throwing the phone across the room.

"Okay, Mike, whatever, but that is what I want. You give me a free ride to the place of my choosing, and I will give you the Medals. That should be simple enough, even for you, Mike."

'That's the deal?"

"That's it. Think we can come to an agreement, Mike, ole' buddy?"

Pryor thought for a moment. "How are we communicating, Clark?"

"Hell, Mike, I got one of these high speed Wal-Mart

disposable phones. The little bastards work great. Got a bunch of them. We can talk all day if you want."

"Jesus Christ, Clark, you're calling this secure line on a disposal cell phone?"

Clark laughed. "Yeah, ain't technology great? Listen, pard, I'm gonna call you back in….let's see…how about thirty minutes? That should give you more than enough time to talk to the main shot-caller. Convince him that I can keep busting you up all day and that it would be in everyone's best interest to do what I say. Got ya by the balls, Mike. Use what little grey matter you have left and recognize it."

"Call me back in thirty minutes, Clark. I'll have an answer."

"God this must be killing you, Mike?"

"You have no idea, asshole what I am feeling. You're a threat to the security of the United Sta…"

"Save it, Mike," interrupted Clark. "Just call your handler and let's make a deal. The sooner I move on, the better. Got it?" He disconnected the call having said what he needed to say. Antagonizing Pryor any longer would be a waste of time.

As he walked down the street, invisible to the traffic and pedestrians, a deep melancholy hit him just above the heart. He realized that soon everything he knew, everything he had tasted, touched, and felt would be gone. Whatever new reality he chose would be just that, a new self - dropped into an environment and time that he would have to deal with. He would be alone, truly alone, cut off from the everyday pace and struggles of this reality. For a moment, he honestly doubted that he could pull off that kind of emotional austerity, that brutal and final severance from all things familiar. And yet as quickly as the feelings of self-doubt and fear washed over him, a renewed sense of resolve and purpose took its place. A small flame of excited anticipation began to flicker.

I can do this, he told himself. He had the upper hand and he intended to keep it. Now all he had to do was think of "where" and most importantly "when" he wanted to go. It was astounding, the feeling that question gave him. Where does a man go when he has all of history lying at his feet? Where indeed.

Chapter Nineteen

The snow was still falling the next morning as Hauser rubbed the sleep from his eyes and slowly sat up. The room was cold enough to see his breath. Looking over, he saw that Campbell was still asleep, barely visible in the blankets of the small bed across the room. They had checked in just before one in the morning and fallen into a dead sleep a short time later. Neither wanted to talk; the cold and the raw emotions of the incident with the police officer had hammered them flat. Now, the only thing Hauser wanted to do was get dressed, get warm, and get some coffee.

"Yo Campbell, time to get up, bro," announced Hauser pulling on his pants. "Let's get some chow. I'm starving." The low rumble of an electric streetcar could be heard going by below the window outside. "Campbell, time to rock. Let's go."

Hauser walked over and nudged Campbell's shoulder, immediately sensing that something was wrong. He slowly pulled back the blanket covering Campbell's head and was shocked to see the wide-eyed ashen face of a dead man. "Jesus," whispered Hauser stepping back, still trying to comprehend the situation.

Hauser knelt down beside the body. There was no blood, no apparent wound, yet here the man was, dead as a stone. Stunned, Hauser leaned closer and lifted each eyelid, the cause of death slowly becoming apparent. While the left pupil appeared to be normal, the right eye had large visible blood spots. Campbell had suffered a brain aneurysm during the night, a condition that probably killed him instantly in his sleep. *He probably had the vascular time bomb ticking away in his head for years*, thought Hauser, gently closing the man's eyes and standing up. "Son of a bitch," he whispered. *What now?* This was a huge complication. The old woman at the desk had seen them together the night before. Once the body was found, he would become the prime suspect, a person of interest at the very least. Mulling over his options he quickly put on his shirt, shoes, and the heavy coat that was still damp from the night before.

He carefully went through Campbell's pockets finding his pistol, the extra magazine, and most importantly, the small plastic return device. He found his wallet and the small leather bound pouch filled with documents of identification and in-country travel certificates. Even the government issuing authority in Berlin would not have been able to tell that they were faked and forged.

Once sure that the body was clear of any identification, he sat back on his bed and tried to think of his next move. In his heart he knew that he would never again get a clear shot at Hitler. The man was too well-protected, and without help any assassination attempt would be certain suicide. His only course of action now was to cut his losses and get back to his time, his reality. He would just have to accept the fact that he had failed, a hard thing for any operator to live with.

Angry that he had no other choice, he stuffed all of Campbell's belongings into his coat pocket and stood up. Thinking that activating the return device in the room was as good a place as any to access the Continuum, he took a deep breath, crouched down with his arms clenched to his chest, closed his eyes, and pushed the activation button. Nothing happened. He stood up shocked as the crushing weight of reality hit him in the heart. Campbell's device would never work. It had been a one-way ticket. If they had somehow been successful in the operation, the people behind Stone Gate would have wanted no witnesses, nobody around that might tell the tale. As a last gesture of hope, he pushed the device button again and waited for that familiar, frigid rush of wind. Nothing happened. The only sounds came from the morning traffic outside on the snow-covered streets.

Oddly calm, he took a deep breath in the cold room and looked over at Campbell's lifeless body, trying to focus on what he should do next. If lucky, he might have a half-hour of lead-time before Campbell's body was found after he left, not a lot of time to clear the area. An option that could buy more time would be to somehow get Campbell's body out of the hotel and dump it in an isolated location. That could slow any kind of investigation considerably.

As an extra precaution, he decided to pay for an extra night in the room. This would keep housekeeping staff away and give him the chance to move the body under the cover of darkness. Hopefully by the time the body was found and any link to him was made, he would be on a ship somewhere headed back to the States.

After paying the four Marks for the extra night, he headed back up the stairs looking for another way to get down to the street. The hotel had a single narrow winding staircase that ended at the fourth floor. Standing in the center of the fourth floor hallway, he recognized that he had several things in his favor. First, the hallways were dimly lit. Second, the floor was carpeted, providing a good sound barrier for movement. And third, his room was at the end of the hall where a folding ceiling door led to the roof. With some effort he would be able to get Campbell's body up to the roof and then, hopefully, drop it over the side to the alley on the backside of the building. It was a macabre way for the operator to go but the only option that had any real chance of success.

Hauser looked around the quiet vacant hallway once more before reaching up and pulling the collapsible ladder down from the ceiling. Quickly climbing up, he saw the white string pull-cord for the single light bulb attached to one of the roof rafters. He turned on the light and spotted, way off to his left, a narrow boardwalk that led to the roof ladder and door. *Hopefully the roof door is unlocked* he thought as he made his way down the walkway and up the short ladder. To his relief, the roof hatch opened easily, giving him a cold blast of snow and wind. Climbing up and onto the large flat snow-covered roof, he made his way to the far edge and looked over. Four floors below lay the vacant alley. *This will work* he thought heading back down.

He would take care of the body, but until then he resolved to document everything that had happened. He had accepted the fact that he was now permanently cut off from his time. Whatever life he had left would be spent in this era, a stranger in an even stranger land. In his mind whatever contract he had with the men that had sent him here had been broken. They had made a decision to not bring him back. He even doubted that Campbell would have been able to return. As a response to this betrayal, he decided to write it all down. He would send the documentation to someone who would read about what had happened. Even if they did not believe it, he would be heard.

After walking back to his room, he sat down on the bed, surprised by the lack of melancholy he felt for what he had lost. Of all his days in all the years of growing up in the present day world of IPhones, laptop computers, and the situational ethics that are the norm of modern life, it was here now that he felt at peace. He had a pervasive sense that he was all right. Despite the tremendous hardship and loss, he knew in his heart that coming here had been a fantastic gift, one that only a handful of men in all of history had experienced.

He knew that if he was going to survive in this new reality that he would have to embrace everything about his new time and place, accept it as his real life. That life would start the moment he dropped Campbell's body off the roof, a strange symbolic act of rebirth, a fitting end and beginning.

Walking up to the window, he noticed that the snow had stopped falling and weak rays of frosted sunshine were trying to push through the scattered overcast. The street below was now filled with trucks, cars, and people bundled deep in coats and scarves.

As he looked over at Campbell's body, the mechanics of what he needed to do now came into focus. This time of day, when most of the rooms were empty and hallway traffic low, might be the best time to get Campbell to the roof. Once that was done he would be able to concentrate on the dissertation he was about to write. Campbell looked to weigh about a hundred and eighty pounds. It would be a dead-weight ball-buster carrying him up two ladders but not impossible. He thought back to BUDS and remembered the midnight beach insertions. He remembered how long he had held up his section of the rubber assault boat back in Coronado. It had been a mind-numbing, backbreaking ordeal that had driven more than a few BUDS classmates to ring out. No, it would be a bitch to fireman-carry the dead man up to the roof, but he knew he could do it. His life depended on it, and that was motivation enough for any man.

Chapter Twenty

Crawford was in his Crystal City office that overlooked the Potomac before dawn. He had received all the latest information on the anomaly and its current destabilized status just after midnight. Sleep had been impossible since then. Shaw, his scientific lead on the project should be arriving anytime with his assessment. According to the preliminary reports massive power fluctuations within the anomaly were making it nearly impossible to regulate and control the massive amount of Gamma ray saturation waves that were being emitted.

Aside from this crisis, he had been called by Pryor less than an hour ago concerning the elimination of the FBI Agent Clark, a man who was somehow eluding the entire active service units of the NSA, the CIA, and the Defense Intelligence Agency with the use of some Magic Medals that he intended to trade for his life and freedom.

A knock on his office door pulled him from his thoughts. "Come in".

Shaw opened the door and tentatively stepped into the large office. "Morning, Sir," he announced walking over to Crawford's massive dark wooden desk.

"Sit down, Shaw," replied Crawford still looking at the papers on his desk. After a moment, Crawford closed the file and looked up with a sigh. "Okay, what is happening with the anomaly?"

Shaw pulled his laptop from his briefcase. "Sir, over the last twelve hours we have seen massive fluctuations of energy within the anomaly and on the peripheral fields. Rad levels within the containment area are within the hazard range, high enough that I have suspended all movement within that specific area. In addition Gamma radiation has been picked up on the slide monitors within the second containment array, also well within the hazard spectrum."

Crawford sat back in his chair. "What about the assets currently downrange? Is there still a link?"

"No, sir," replied Shaw shaking his head. "The energy surges are far too great. We have lost all ability to monitor any of the individuals currently within the system. None of the bio regulators are online. We have even lost the basic light spectrum indicators which is something we did not expect."

"So what is our course of action as of this morning?" questioned Crawford.

"Well sir, as you would expect, my whole team is currently at the facility going over the data. We should have some clear indication about what's going on within a few hours."

Crawford thought for a moment. "How dangerous is our current position?"

"Sir, that's difficult to quantify. I am not sure…"

"It's a simple question, Doctor Shaw," interrupted Crawford. "I expect a simple answer. How high is our risk?"

"Extreme, sir. We have never seen these kinds of power spikes."

Crawford nodded. "All right, based on what we know now, what's your preliminary assessment?"
Shaw closed his laptop, gathering his thoughts. "Sir, I honestly feel that if we cannot control the power fluctuations,

we need to cut all power to the anomaly - all of it. We would have to go dark."

Crawford shook his head. "I really don't think that would be our best course of action, Doctor. We currently have people involved in an operation that could possibly change the course of history as we know it. Do I need to remind you of that fact?"

Shaw could feel the blood draining from his face. The last thing he wanted to do was start an argument with a man who could have him killed even before he left the building, and he was on very thin ice.

"Sir, if we cannot get control of the massive amount of dark matter that is within a light beam width away from the containment array, the results could be catastrophic. And as far as the men who were sent, there is no way for us to get them back. The last power spike scrambled all of the return indicators and laser monitors. We could not bring them back if we wanted to. They're gone."

Crawford smiled without humor. "I'm not sure you realize what's at stake here, Doctor. We have had power spikes before, have we not? I thought we had this same problem when we stopped the President's assassination last March."

"Not to this level. Not this prolonged. It really is unprecedented."

"And you think this could work itself into a *catastrophic* condition as you say?"

Shaw held Crawford's gaze. "Sir, what I am saying is that if these erratic power fluctuations continue, we could lose control of the containment field which means we could lose control of the anomaly."

Crawford stood up from his desk and walked over to the large picture window. "Do what you have to do, Shaw," he replied looking out over the river. "But keep the power on. The mission may still have a chance even if the first two fail. I want to be able to send more through." He turned and faced Shaw. "Are we clear, Doctor?"

Shaw nodded knowing full well that the discussion was over. "Yes, sir, I understand. With all due respect, I would like to submit my resignation. Maybe you need someone better qualified to run the program. I'm not sure I can meet your expectations."

"This wouldn't be a left-handed bit of blackmail would it, Doctor Shaw? I think you know perfectly well how valuable you are to this program."

Shaw took a deep breath. "Sir, as a scientist it is my duty to be as intellectually honest as possible with you concerning my deep skepticism about the current safety of the program."

"Have you lost faith in what we are trying to do here?" The hard edge in Crawford's voice was clear.

"No, Sir, not in the least. My concern is that if we do not address this power problem, we may not have a program to manage."

Crawford turned back to the window. "I think we're done here, Doctor. Your resignation request is denied. My suggestion is that you focus your full attention on keeping the program running at all cost. Please don't make me regret bringing you to this project." Crawford turned around and smiled, again without humor. "Keep me posted, Doctor Shaw."

In Shaw's mind, he knew that no matter what he told Crawford, Stone Gate would not be shut down or even limited in its scope, no matter how dire the predictions concerning its safety. This dangerous dance with the forces of the universe was going to continue. As he walked out of Crawford's office, he could not remember a time when he felt this out-matched by circumstance.

Crawford and the rest of the men that controlled Stone Gate were blinded by the power, the influence it wielded and deaf to the cries of caution. Hubris - the Achilles heal of all men.

Chapter Twenty-One

Clark walked a solid ten blocks away from the Starbucks before ducking into one of the local coffee shops behind a group of Japanese tourists. He headed to the back of the busy café, carefully moving through the rush of waitresses and bus boys. In the large restroom he found an empty stall, stepped inside and removed the Medallion.

Collecting himself, he took a deep breath and stepped out of the stall, instantly feeling an over-powering sense of vulnerability. He stood under the unforgiving fluorescent lights, staring at his image above the sink, shocked by what he saw.

Stepping close to the mirror, he was stunned to see that his hair had turned almost totally grey. His face looked like he had aged ten years. "Good God," he whispered out-loud, rubbing the three-day stubble on his chin. *What is going on?* Stepping away from his reflection, he instinctively knew that the Medals, for all their power, were taking a toll on his physical body. Their prolonged use was causing him to age at an accelerated rate.

He quickly walked through the busy café and stepped outside into the cold sunshine, determined now more than ever to finish this. A half a block down the street he walked into a narrow alley that was lined with bright green recycling bins and stacks of bundled cardboard, a clear example of the anal-retentive, uber environment-conscious culture that seemed to be pervasive throughout the Northwest.

He took a seat on one of the cardboard bundles and punched in Pryor's phone number. "Yo, Mike, as promised I am calling back. You ready to make a deal?"
"Bad news, asshole. There is no deal," replied Pryor as he

walked up the steps of the Forestall Building in downtown DC. "Talked to my superiors and they said you pose a grave and present threat to the security of the United States and do not merit any kind of deal. Like I said, Clark, you're a dead man. You just haven't' fallen down yet."

Clark shook his head. "So you are going to play this thing out. You know where I am going next?"

"Go anywhere you want, pal. It makes no difference. I have a signed DIC elimination letter with your name on it on my desk, and that's all I need to know."

Clark thought for a moment. "Okay, Pryor, if that's how you want to play this thing out, you got it."

"Hey, Clark, what happened to the tough guy banter?" asked Pryor. "All that first name basis bullshit? Hell, you sound like someone who just got kicked in the nuts. C'mon, Agent, let's see how much leverage you really have. Give us your best shot."

"You're a fool, Pryor," he replied, disconnecting the call. It was pointless talking anymore. It was clear that the operatives that had chased him in the helicopter in Idaho had not reported to higher what they had seen. The only thing he had presented to Pryor was his ability to avoid being picked up on the street. No real manifest magic there.

In order for him to really get Pryor's attention he would have to confront the man face to face. A mind-blowing, visual aid just might do the trick. Now all he had to do was travel twenty-six hundred miles without the use of a car or a plane and not get himself killed in the process. Sounded easy enough.

****

"The structure of space time, as cosmologists estimate today, consists of about 70 to 75% of dark energy, 20 to 25% of dark matter, and 5% of ordinary matter (this last includes the visible stars and galaxies of the universe." (Maroun center for quantum physics)

Shaw reread the passage a second time trying to figure out what he was missing in his calculations. The hard truth at the core was that the Continuum was deteriorating, dissolving within the realms of manageable fusion and basic reactor energy. It simply could not be sustained at this level, and for all his intellectual reasoning, he did not know why. Adding to his growing frustration was his need to convince people like Crawford of the very real and growing danger about what they were doing and the possible catastrophic consequences of doing nothing.

He had gone back to the lab directly after his meeting with the DIC and was now reviewing the latest phasing array data with two other physicists, men who had been up for the last twenty-four hours working the numbers. Jim Caswell, a highly respected nuclear physicist on loan to Stone Gate from Livermore Labs, dropped his glasses on the table and sat back in his chair with an exhausted sigh. "Do these people really understand the danger here?" he announced, shaking his head. "I mean we are dealing with off-the-scale cosmic forces."

Tim Halberd, a noted Quantum physics expert from Cal Tech, slid the latest graph sheet across the table to Shaw. "Take a look at table five, Hammond. Those numbers on the residue output are in real time. We are way past the critical on this. We have to shut down. My recommendation would be within the hour."
Shaw looked at the sheet as an involuntary shiver ran down his back, something he had never experienced before. "My

God," he whispered, "you say these calculations are in real time?"

Halberd nodded solemnly. "Yep, and unless something is done and done quickly, I am going to get as far away from this facility as fast as my car will go. I suggest you do the same."

Shaw sat back in his chair. "I don't think we need to panic here, Tim. We need to figure out a solution to the flux problem. We have had similar things like this before."

Halberd leaned forward, locking Shaw with a hard flat gaze. "Nobody is in a panic, Hammond. We are simply telling you that this is now unsustainable and that we are risking a Dark Matter interaction. You know perfectly well how devastating that would be. You have to shut down. We are losing containment by the hour. The northeast grid has already had two micro-blackouts because of the drain we are pulling, and that's just to stay even."

Shaw studied the rest of the report. "What about Deuterium levels?"

"Low," replied Caswell. "As Tim said, we are just trying to stay even. The pumps are running at full capacity."

It was at this moment that the crushing weight of decision and consequence fell. "I ah, I don't know if you guys fully understand the consequences of shutting down the program," replied Shaw sitting back in his chair. "I mean, not to be overly dramatic here, but I was instructed *not* to shut down by the highest authority."

"Jesus, Hammond, if we lose control of this thing there is no telling how much damage it can do. I mean there is a greater good here to consider. There really is."

"I understand that, Tim, I do. I also know that we have two assets still downrange that we need to contact and hopefully get back. What is our responsibility to those men? If we shut down, there is no way for a recalibration on our side. What then?"

"They're gone, Hammond," replied Caswell softly. "Eight hours ago a plasma surge pushed all the beacons to default, the bio scans, everything. We lost vectors, E-mag rhythms. Even the laser designators went off the scale. They're gone. It would take weeks of online recalibration to even get close, time we just do not have. Hell, boss, we are down to hours."

Shaw thought for a moment and then nodded to the two men he trusted most within the Stone Gate project. "Go. Take the data you have and leave the facility. I will keep things running here for as long as I can."

"Hammond, you can't do tha.."

"Not a request, Tim," interrupted Shaw. "It's an order. Go home and get your families as far away from DC as you can."

"You cannot be serious, Hammond?" Caswell replied. "If you do not shut this down, you will have a catastrophic reaction. It's suicide-plain and simple."

Shaw nodded. "I understand, fellas, but I want you to do what I say. Take the rest of the staff with you. Go on, go home to your families."

"What about the surrounding area?" asked Caswell, standing. "There has got to be at least a couple thousand people working in different buildings just yards from here. What's our responsibility to them?"

"Tim, go home," replied Shaw. "Just go home. I am doing all I can."

Halberd slowly scooped up his notes and stood up. "You're going to need help with this, boss. I'm staying. You can take your orders and shove 'em up your ass. How's that for insubordination?"

Shaw smiled. "Pretty good. You sure you know what you're doing?"

Halberd laughed while loading his briefcase. "Yeah, probably more than you do, boss, and I'm sure the rest of the staff feels the same way."

Caswell nodded before he turned to leave. "I'm staying too. Always wanted to see what the end of the world looked like. Now's my chance."

Chapter Twenty-Two

Getting Campbell's body to the roof hadn't been as difficult as anticipated, Hauser thought, walking down the front steps of the hotel. It was just after eleven o'clock in the morning, and the only thing on his mind now as he stepped out onto the street was to get as far away from Munich as possible. He had been able to fireman-carry Campbell's body up the first and second ladder and then put him behind one set of the tall chimneys on the far side of the expansive roof. He had reconsidered dropping the body into the alley, deciding instead to leave him hidden there, where weeks might pass before he was discovered. The temperatures at night were well below freezing and would hide the smell of decay. When the body was eventually discovered showing no signs of visible injury, it would be presumed that he had gone to the roof for unknown reasons, had a stroke, and died. There would be no identification on the corpse, nothing that would tell anyone who this man was or where he had come from. Campbell would be folded up into the pages of history, just one more nameless body in a legion of unidentified dead with no next-of-kin inquiries.

Ahead, just to the left of the large red and black Nazi swastika banner that ruffled in the cold breeze, Hauser spotted the yellow and black BAHNOF sign pointing towards the train station. He crossed the street, a frigid gust of wind at his back quickening his step. He needed to put as much time and distance as he could between him and the city. Just before walking down into the tunnel that led to the trains, he spotted a small book and stationary store off to the left. He crossed the street as heavy trucks rumbled by carrying everything from beer barrels to beef.

He stepped into the shop, a small bell tinkling over the

doorframe. He stood just inside letting the comforting smell of pipe smoke and newspapers wash over him. It felt wonderful getting out of the cold.

An old man, who had been sitting behind the counter slowly stood up. "Guten Morgen," he announced smiling. "Wie kann ich dir helfen?"

Taking off his gloves, Hauser stepped up to the counter. "Ah, I need some writing paper and a couple of pens," he replied in German. The old man nodded and carefully pulled a small box of paper and several pens out from under the glass counter. "I am also going to need a large mailing envelope," he said, pulling several Duetsche Marks out of his pocket.

The old man nodded and placed the items in a paper sack. "That will be two Marks."

Hauser handed over the money. "Do you sell stamps here?" he asked, immediately regretting the question. Everyone knew that in the Thirties only the post office sold stamps. It was a stupid slip of the tongue.

The old man smiled. "No, the Post sells them. Two blocks down," he replied pointing towards the door.

Gathering his purchase, Hauser nodded, thanked the old man, and then left the shop as quickly as he could. It was careless questions like that that raised suspicion, made him memorable, and that was the last thing he needed to be. As he stepped outside into the cold air, he swore to himself to be more careful, more watchful of what he said. He was far from being clear of danger. Even the most innocent nuance of mannerism or speech could mark him as different - could get him killed.

He was now on the run with no real proof of who he was or where he was from. Odds were not in his favor that he would even make it out of Germany. There were countless check points along with random police and army patrols just looking for people who did not fit the location or the event, men with guns and the authority to use them. Street justice was now the norm, and for his continued survival, the devil was truly in the details.

Trying to remain as calm as possible, he walked down the steps of the station tunnel passing numerous soldiers walking up and down the wide stairway. They carried themselves with swaggering confidence, the same look every young untested soldier carries, youthful warriors in the prime of physical life, totally unaware of the horrors of war that awaited them just months from now.

After waiting in the short line, he stepped up to the small ticket box and slid a Ten Duetch Mark bill under the glass. "One for Bremanhaven, please," he said in German. The pretty blonde haired girl behind the glass smiled and snapped a ticket out of her ledger, stamped it, and slid it under the glass. He had timed the move just right as a line of people had quickly formed behind him, all loaded down with coats and bags and small-wheeled luggage carts. He checked his ticket just as the 7:30 morning train rumbled into the station, hissing great billowing clouds of steam like some huge lumbering beast. He had never seen a working steam engine up close, much less ride on one. In fact, when he thought about it, he could count on one hand the number of times he had actually ridden on a train anywhere. The hiss and steam of the engine, the bustling crowd, and the general ambiance of the place gave the platform a surreal vibe, like some extravagant movie set. It was life in all its rawness and hope. A hundred smells, a thousand sounds all coming together in that familiar organized chaos of human movement.
Strangely enough, it felt good to be part of the crush, part of the herd. It was the first time in days that he didn't feel the emotional pain of being separate, different. As he climbed the

short flight of stairs onto the train, he felt the tension in his back and neck start to ease. He was no longer on a mission, no longer under the sharp-edged rules of a lethal plan. The weight of success or failure no longer plagued his every waking moment. That burden had been lifted the microsecond he had pushed the return activator and nothing happened. He had been written off, cut loose from all things familiar. In a strange way, it gave him a sense of emotional freedom he had never experienced before.

He slowly made his way down the narrow aisle reading the door numbers on the compartments. "Twenty-six," he whispered out loud stopping at the highly polished door. This would be home for the next six and a half hours. Hopefully, whoever would be sharing his compartment would not be much of a talker. He wanted this time to decompress. He wanted to be free from guarded speech and protected lies.

It was exhausting carrying on a normal conversation with someone when in the back of your mind you were thinking of fifteen ways to kill the person. He stepped into the small compartment and tossed his knapsack on the long wide seat that faced the direction the train would be going. The last thing he wanted was to get motion sickness by riding backwards for six hours. He sat down with a sigh just as the compartment door opened up and a young uniformed soldier stepped in. He smiled and nodded. "Gotten Tag," he announced setting his large rucksack on the other bench.

"Good Morning," replied Hauser in German, instantly knowing that somehow, somewhere along the trip, this young soldier was going to be a problem. There would be conversation, there would be curiosity, and then there would be trouble, the kind of trouble that has a man washing the blood off his hands at three o'clock in the morning. *Christ,* thought Hauser, nodding to the soldier as he sat down, *it is going to be a long six and a half hours. It is sad that the young man*

143

will be dead before the real shooting war begins, killed in his sleep, his dreams of honor and glory in conflict cut short between heart beats.

Hauser watched as the young man settled in, unpacking what looked like a couple of hard rolls of bread from his knapsack. He unwrapped the wax paper and handed one to Hauser smiling. "Here, I have two, breakfast," he announced.

Hauser nodded. "Danke. Are you sure? I don't want to eat all your food."

The soldier laughed. "I have plenty. I have a tin of jam in here somewhere," he said rummaging through the pack. "I cannot eat bread without jam."

Before Hauser could answer, there was a gentle knock at the door. "Tickets, please. Tickets." The dark blue uniformed conductor leaned in smiling. "Good morning. Tickets, please."

The man click-punched the small strips of paper and then left the compartment, his call for tickets trailing him down the hall. For Hauser, watching the simple acts of normal people in everyday life was beginning to draw powerful emotions. People were doing the same things that people in his time were doing; nothing had changed except the clothing. They laughed, they ate, they conversed, they walked and moved through their existence with a familiar ease. Here, he was starting to see the deep grooves of a civilized world, greased by the hopes, the dreams, and the desires all humans share. Unsettled by this new perception, he sat back in his seat as the station outside slowly started to roll by.

As the train picked up speed, Hauser knew that with each passing second he was melting deeper into this new reality, this new self. The train had become a metaphor for his life, he was traveling to the unknown, where all the rules of survival could change by the hour.

As he ate the bread and jam, the question of what his father would think of all this suddenly flashed through his mind, and with it a physical jolt as he realized that his father was now just *two years old*, living somewhere in Sacramento, California. "Holy shit," he whispered under his breath. *Holy shit indeed.*

Chapter Twenty- Three

After having stopped by the large Wal-Mart on his way out of town, Clark had used the rest-stop restroom to change into the long johns and the close fitting ski jacket and now carefully packed a backpack with the supplies he would need for his flight. He had also picked up gloves, a skateboard helmet, and a strong pair of goggles. He was ready. He took the GPS out of the package, filled the battery container, and turned it on.

The highway rest stop had the appearance of a small but well-groomed park with old growth shade trees and picnic tables. Clark had picked a table farthest from the large parking lot, not wanting to be too cavalier with his ability to escape whoever was trying to kill him.

Sitting under the trees on a cool but sunny afternoon, he knew that no matter what he did to demonstrate his ability concerning the Medals, Pryor would never back off; he would never quit. Men like that never did, meat eaters, alpha males who took losing at anything as a deeply personal affront. Even faced with an unbeatable obstacle, these types continued to fight, continued on the chosen path even if that path would lead to certain destruction.

The only obvious way to stop Pryor was to remove him from the equation. There was no other option, and even that might not work. After all, Pryor was just a small cog in a very big and dangerous wheel. No, if all of this were ever going to stop, Stone Gate's main shot-caller would also have to be dealt with. When he thought about it, he realized that he now had the power to become the hunter. If he was smart and had a little bit of luck on his side, he just might get through this in one piece.

Looking around just to make sure no one was paying any

attention, he pulled the smaller bag out of his larger backpack and carefully started removing the contents. He had at least seventy thousand dollars in cash - seven rubber band-bound stacks of ten thousand dollars each, the blue velvet Crown Royal bag with the two medals and Robashow's tattered blue leather notebook. He stuffed the contents back in the bag, confident that he had the means and the ability to complete his plan. He had decided to fly to Robashaw's first way-point, clearly marked with a GPS Lat /Long in the note book. He programmed the numbers in on the GPS and then pulled out the Triple AAA Washington State travel map. Checking the distance against the GPS, he estimated his first camp to be a solid two hundred and eighty miles almost due East. If he could keep a fairly consistent airspeed of seventy-five miles per hour and could stay on heading, he would be in the area in about four hours.

He checked his watch. It was just after one in the afternoon. There would be more than ample time to get where he needed to be before the sun went down. Looking over his shoulder, he spotted a good place to take off, a large flat open space, clear of trees and power lines, that ran a good fifty yards before ending at a chain link fence.

Several years ago he had taken a few small-fixed wing-flying lessons at his wife's urging while stationed in Albuquerque. Now, as he sat working up the courage to actually leave the ground, he found himself mentally approaching the trip as a fixed wing pilot would prior to take off.

He stuffed the notebook back in his backpack and took a deep breath. As he zipped up his jacket and pulled on the gloves, he suddenly became aware of a small boy around the age of ten holding a large dog on a leash in the area. The dog seemed in a great hurry to sniff and pee at the base of every tree in the park. Clark nodded to the kid as he tightened the wrist strap of his GPS.

"Why you wearing those gloves and coat?" he asked tugging the dog's leash. "It's not cold out."

Jesus, thought Clark. *Now what? Where did this kid come from anyway?* "I ah, I'm sick, so I need to stay warm. Where are your parents?"

"In the bathroom with my sister. We're from Ohio. We're on vacation. Are you on vacation?" he asked, suddenly jerked sideways by the big dog.

Clark shook his head, picking up his helmet and goggles. "Look, kid, you need to go see your parents. I'm pretty sick, so you need to stay away, okay?"

"What's wrong with you? I had chicken pox last month. You ever had chicken pox?"

Just as Clark was about to answer, a short heavyset woman holding the hand of a young girl shouted in their direction. "Robert, let's go! Get over here."

"Okay!" he shouted back. "Bandit hasn't pooped yet. That's my dog's name, Bandit. I named him. Do you have a dog?"

"Robert, let's go! Now!" shouted the woman angrily.

"Your mom sounds mad. You better get going."

"Yeah, she always yells." He jerked the leash just as the dog was dropping a thick pile of crap. "C'mon, Bandit. C'ya, mister!" he shouted, pulling the dog along.

"C'ya, kid."

As he trotted and tried to squat, the big lab dropped small

piles of shit all the way to the sidewalk, a sight that made Clark chuckle. He had always liked kids, had always thought he would have some when the job finally settled down. A sharp melancholy hit him just above the heart as he realized that whatever sunset-colored dreams he had of a loving wife and children probably would never happen.

Shaking off the images of something he would never have, he buttoned the chinstrap and tightened the shoulder straps of his backpack. "Stay focused," he whispered out loud. "Stay in the game."

Looking around one last time, he walked out into the clearing, lowering his goggles. He checked the GPS, took a deep breath, and then took off in a dead sprint. In five steps he jumped into his now familiar superman pose and just as quickly thudded to the ground with a grunt. Stunned, he rolled to his knees, only to remember that talking to the kid had distracted him from putting on the Gold Medal. It was still in his backpack. Feeling like a complete and very visible idiot, he ripped the pack off his back and dug out the Gold Medallion. He draped the chain over his head and tucked it under his jacket, immediately feeling the heavy medal suck down to his chest.

He quickly got to his feet and took off running towards the fence, not really caring if anyone had seen him or not. He was greatly relieved when he dove with arms outstretched and held height off the ground, his body clearing the fence by two feet. He straightened his back and stiffened his legs, increasing his speed, the wind rushing by the ear holes of his helmet. He laughed out loud as he continued to climb, the air growing colder by the second. Rolling his wrist slightly he was able to see the GPS and the purple direction indicator line. Adjusting slightly to his left put him exactly on the heading he needed to be. He could see clear terrain features now, and the biting cold at the speed and altitude were no longer a factor with the upgrade of the long johns and goggles.

According to the GPS he was going eighty-three miles an hour, at an altitude of twenty-seven hundred feet, not exactly aircraft speed, but fast enough at this pace to get him to the waypoint long before dark.

As Clark flew he had to remind himself that this was no dream, no drug or booze induced hallucination; he was actually flying. The power and exhilaration of the experience was almost emotionally overwhelming. At the same time, the actual mechanics of flight seemed to be becoming easier by the second. Adjusting direction by moving the head slightly, increasing or decreasing speed with the legs were all movements that were becoming natural, oddly second nature.

Far below, through the haze he could see the green and brown patchwork of fields and crops clearly bordered by straight dirt roads, fences, and black asphalt. The panorama to the horizon was an incredible sight, awe inspiring in it's scope and grandeur.

He had not been much on church or even organized religion for that matter, but this experience, this mind-blowing endeavor hit a very spiritual cord. *Why was this allowed to happen? More importantly, why was I allowed to be the recipient of this experience?* These questions rolled through his mind on a loop, unanswered. He could not shake the growing unease, a feeling that he was not worthy of these medallions and the power they gave, and the more he used them, the stronger the feeling grew.

He adjusted his course slightly after looking at the GPS and discovered, to his surprise, that he had already flown close to eighty miles. It was amazing how much ground he could cover so quickly. Low and off to his left he watched as a small plane kept a steady course almost parallel to his. For a fleeting second he seriously thought about dropping down next to the plane, letting the pilot and passengers see him. He laughed out loud as he thought about the looks he would get flying unassisted just beyond the wings tips. He could only imagine the utter shock and disbelief at the incomprehensible sight of a man wearing a skateboard helmet and goggles in free flight - staggering, terrifying.

Deciding against the bad idea of exposing himself unnecessarily, he planed his hands and gained another six hundred feet of altitude, well above and out of the line-of-sight of anyone in the plane. He knew that changing a person's perceptions of reality could be a dicey proposition. The deep ruts and grooves of mental stability could not accept an image that defied everything ever known about the material world. Sanity would be questioned. A fear of losing control would not be far behind which could lead to equally irrational behavior. No, on second thought, flying down next to a fully occupied aircraft might not be the best of ideas. Besides, he was confidant that all aviation and law enforcement radio channels in the area were being monitored. Anything out of the ordinary would be reported and acted upon. He was already getting tired and did not want to spend the rest of the afternoon trying to evade an NSA helicopter.

As Clark made another course correction and gained another three hundred feet, he knew in his gut that it was only a matter of time until the powers that be recognized that what he was doing was something so extraordinary, so classified, and so dangerous that every asset at their disposal would be thrown at him. This thought was a quick reminder that he wasn't as smart or ahead of the game as he had believed; he had drawn first blood, and now they would be coming after him with a vengeance. There would be no mercy.

Chapter Twenty-Four

For Hauser, sitting in the small train compartment trying not to make small talk was proving to be very difficult. The young German seemed intent on carrying on a conversation and was now taking sips of mint schnapps from a small flask, a flask he was almost demanding Hauser share.

"So what do you do?" he asked, slumping back in his seat as he unbuttoned the neck of his tunic.

"I am a pipe fitter."

The German smiled and took another sip. "I don't believe you," he replied wiping his mouth with his sleeve.

Hauser felt the hair on the back of his neck stand up. "Yeah, why is that?"

The German leaned forward, his brow furrowed in mock concern. "Your accent. You sound like one of my teachers from school." Hauser could see that the strong alcohol was having an effect; his face was flushed and his voice was getting louder.

Hauser smiled. "Is that good or bad?"

The German sat back, a memory taking all expression from his face. "Both, he was a good teacher, but he annoyed me. He was a pompous ass." He leaned forward again close enough for the schnapps on his breath to cross the space between them. "You see, my father was a very hard working man," announced the German sternly. "He worked in a pot factory all his life."

As Hauser listened he was already trying to think of how he

was going to kill him. He looked to be in his late twenties, maybe a hundred and seventy pounds. He was left handed, so the punches would be coming from his right in a fistfight. His neck was thin. He didn't fill out the shoulders of the uniform so he probably did not have a lot of upper body strength. His thin wire-rimmed glasses would smash into the face when the punches started. He had been drinking heavily from the flask since they pulled out of the station so his timing and motor skills would be highly impaired. To Hauser, the German would be no match. It would be over in seconds.

When the time was right, Hauser would clip him with a ripping upper cut knocking him senseless and then put him in a carotid chokehold until he was dead. It would be quiet and there would be no blood. The worst part would be that he would most likely shit and piss himself, a smell that would be hard to hide, especially in the small train compartment.

"And he worked at that terrible job just so I could go to the best school," continued the German. "He was not an educated man, just a man who worked hard for his family." He took another drink from the flask, his eyes starting to tear. "I loved my father," he said sitting back.

Hauser looked at the large window, trying to see if it would open wide enough to push a body through.

"That teacher, that piece of shit teacher had an educated accent just like yours," he said smiling without the slightest bit of humor. "He used to say that anyone who did not have educated parents was doomed from childhood and would only be able to do menial labor like working in factories and such." He leaned forward again his eyes squinted in anger. "How could a man say something like that to a room full of working class children?"
And then again, he thought, *I might just shoot the German in the chest. Hopefully the bullet would not go through him, the seat, and*

hit someone in the next compartment. The suppressed shot would only put out around eighty decibels, a report well-covered by the rumbling of the train. Still, there was that possible over-penetration problem. Christ, this was going to be harder than I thought.

"So you see, and I mean no offense to you, Mister pipe fitter, but your accent has brought up a memory of a man I hated. Here have a drink."

Hauser took the flask and then faked taking a sip. "Thank you. Sorry for bringing up bad memories."

The German sat back with a sigh. "No, no, it's not you. I just miss my father. He died last year."

"I'm sorry to hear that."

The man looked as if he were about to cry. "Fucking influenza killed him in three weeks. Almost took my sister," he said, his voice barely a whisper. "So, pipe fitter, what is your name?" he asked, suddenly pulling himself out of the sad memory.

Shit, here come the questions. This is how it starts. Why didn't this son of a bitch just drink quietly and pass out. It would make what was soon to happen so much easier. "Ah, my name is Hauser, Jacob Hauser and you?"

The German leaned forward extending his hand. "Edmond Kraus. My pleasure. So why are you going to Brenhaven? You have family there?"

Hauser shook his head. "No, looking for work in the shipyards. They say they need a thousand men to weld. So I am going." It was a rehearsed lie but one that sounded solid on the surface. The German government was retooling its factory and war fighting capability, and ship building in the deep-water port of Brenhaven was very active. The man seemed satisfied with the lie.

"What about you? Why are you traveling?"

Krauss smiled and took another sip from the flask. "I have a two week pass. My sister and her new husband live in Brenhaven. She just had a baby." He raised his flask in a toast. "I am an uncle now."

Hauser smiled and extended his hand. "Congratulations, you'll make a great uncle. Are you married? Do you have a family?"

Krauss laughed. "No, thank God. My mistress is the Army. I doubt a wife would put up with that arrangement. You?"

Hauser shook his head. "No, cannot find a woman who would put up with me."

Krauss raised his flask again. "We should drink to the women who would not have us. Their loss," he laughed and took a long drink. "You know, Jacob, I am still confused by your accent. Where did you say you were from?" He was now slurring his words.

"A lot of places. I follow the work."

Krauss nodded. "Yes, but where did you go to school?" The question had an edge to it.

Hauser had decided upon a basal skull fracture, a maneuver that would separate the skull from the spinal column. If done right, death would be almost instantaneous. He went over the moves in his head that he had learned in advanced combatives class back at DEV GROUP.

"Ah, hey is there any more schnapps in that flask?"

Krauss shook the flask and smiled. "Sorry, my friend, only enough left for me." He drank down the last bit and then tossed the flask on the pack by his feet. "So, Jacob, how come you are not in the Army? Germany needs every strong man it can get. You look fit."

Hauser could see where this was going. In his drunkenness the German was becoming more belligerent. If this kept up, he would soon be outright hostile. Better to end this now instead of letting it get any worse. It was evident that Krauss had sized him up as some kind of civilian slacker, and now with a head full of liquor, his disdain was coming to the surface.

Hauser slowly took off his overcoat and rolled up the sleeves of his shirt, just in case the German vomited as he was dying. He took a deep breath and then another. Krauss leaned forward, his eyes bloodshot, tinged with an edge of mocking hostility. Krauss was a mean drunk, probably had been his whole young life.

"What do you do in the Army, Krauss? What's your job skill?"

Krauss smiled and then stuck a finger into his left nostril blowing the right one clear on the compartment floor. "I am Infantry but have put in my papers to go to the SS."

Hauser leaned close to Krauss. "You know, my friend, you just made my job a whole lot easier."

"Really, how is that?"

"Well, I think that with your type of personality, Krauss, the SS is going to accept you with open arms. That is something I really cannot let happen. You see, the SS are the biggest, over-the-top, scum-sucking assholes this world has ever seen and you want to be part of that sickness!"

Krauss sat back trying to digest what he had just heard. "What are you saying? Are you trying to provoke me, pipefitter?"

Hauser stood up. "No, dumb ass, I am telling you that I am about to end your life. I just wanted to let you know my true feelings before I did it. You are a soldier so I owe you that much."

Krauss laughed. "Sit down before I...."

Those were the last words that cleared his throat before Hauser dove into him with all the force he could muster. The German's head slammed into the wall of the compartment, instantly knocking him unconscious. He slumped onto his side as Hauser quickly positioned himself at the man's back, wrapping Kraus's head and neck in a firm chokehold. Pushing his weight forward and pulling his feet up on the seat in a crouched position, he was now ready to finish the task. With all his strength, he pushed off the seat standing Krauss upright and then jumped slightly backwards letting his full weight slam onto the German's neck. Hauser felt and heard a dull snap against his arm, followed by an involuntary shudder as the once hopeful SS candidate died. It was the second man he had killed this way in as many days.

As he laid the body length-wise back on the seat and covered him with one of the blankets that had been stored in the overhead rack, he rationalized the killing as necessary, something that needed to be done for the sake of his mission. But as he sat back down, he knew that was a lie. There was no mission. He had failed and now all he was doing was trying to stay alive. The motivation and mission for the "greater good" had died the moment he failed to take the shot he had been sent to take.

Sitting in the over-heated train compartment with a dead man was not the worst of it. He was lying to himself and accepting the justification. He was nothing more than an assassin on the run and deserved nothing more than any other killer. Maybe that's what bothered him the most. Maybe that's all he had ever been. Maybe.

Chapter Twenty- Five

It had been surprisingly easy to hit Robashaw's waypoint. The GPS had been spot-on, putting him within feet of the small clearing on the backside of a ridge that trailed off into the Idaho foothills. This time he landed easily, gently drifting down into the ankle high grass. As he touched down, the wind came up bringing a cold bite to the air.

It had taken him just over four hours to get here, a good travel time marker for future flights and distances. He took off his helmet, goggles, and backpack and sat down in the sweet grass, feeling an intense fatigue wash over him. It was amazing how strenuous it really was flying. Holding a stretched-out body position against the wind for the four hours had given him pain in spots he had never hurt before. He checked his watch and then pulled the notebook out of his pack.

After he had taken a second to absorb his surroundings, the only thing he could hear and see was the wind blowing through the grass and a jet leaving a silent contrail thousands of feet above him. Robashaw had picked his spots well. Turning the well-worn pages of the diary, he wondered how many times the old man had sat here pondering the nature of it all, walking the same emotional tight rope he was on.

The sun would be down in two hours giving him just enough time to find Robashaw's cache and hopefully something to eat. Turning to the waypoint notes, Clark read Robashaw's notation: ***"Looking due East from GPS coordinates 349871, go ten paces."***

Clark turned the GPS due East and started walking. "One, two, three," he said out loud as he stepped off the distance.

"Four, five, six, seven, eight, nine, ten." Looking down, he spotted a small blue scrap of paper sticking out of the grass. He knelt down, surprised to see that it was the edge of a blue plastic tarp that had been exposed by wind and rain. "I'll be damned," he whispered pulling up a large section of the tarp.

After some tugging, he exposed what looked to be a six-foot long and three-foot wide homemade wooden door lying flush to the ground. Raising the door, he discovered a large hole stacked nearly to the top with canned goods and camping supplies wrapped in plastic. He unwrapped a small one-man tent, several tightly wrapped blankets, an axe, and several rolls of toilet paper. It must have taken months for Robashaw to amass and hide what appeared to be several weeks' worth of supplies.

He quickly pulled out the tent and blankets and looked around for a flat spot to set up for the night as the sun was going down and it was getting cold fast. By the time the last of the purple light rays blinked on the horizon, he had his tent set up and was warming up the can of pork and beans over a small cooking fire. Along with the beans he had found several small cans of pineapple in heavy syrup and, to his surprise, a bottle of Coors beer. It wasn't exactly a five-star meal, but he could not remember a time when a beer had tasted better.

That night as he lay wrapped in his blankets listening to the night wind gust across the side of the tent, his mind drifted to another time when he had lain bone-tired under canvas with the sweet smell of mountain sage drifting through the air. He had been with his wife, Donna. They had gone to Yosemite in California four years ago and had been toying with the idea of someday walking the full John Muir trail, a two hundred and eleven-mile trek that started in the uplands of Yosemite and ended at the base of Mount Whitney. Thinking back to those wonderful soft-colored days, Clark had known that the John Muir hike would likely never happen. He couldn't have cared less about walking two hundred miles just for the sake of doing it. Going on camping trips with her, willingly sleeping on rocky ground, and being eaten alive by mosquitos had been for one reason. He had camped to make her happy.

Donna had loved being outdoors, loved cooking over an open fire and taking endless pictures of mountain flowers, chipmunks, and the wide-open vistas. In the end, whatever he could do to make her smile he did gladly. At night with the cool breeze carrying the scent of pine through their tent, they would lie close laughing and talking for hours about all the things married people who are deeply in love talk about. They spoke of things they wanted to see, places they wanted to go, of plans for the future, a future as bright and full of promise as the stars in a clear night sky.

Clark smiled as he remembered that even with all her enthusiasm for camping Donna would not get up to pee unless he held the flashlight. It was just one of her endearing quirks that she was terrified of squatting over a snake. It was one of a million things that made her so special. She had been tough and confident in her professional life yet vulnerable and incredibly feminine when she was around him. He was sure that very few people really saw that side of her - the best side.

He rolled deep into his blankets letting the soft memories of her drift away. There alone in the dark, it would be easy to give in to the loneliness and the despair of the circumstances he was now in. By day physical movement kept the mental demons of doubt and debilitating fear at bay. But here in the dark he had time to ponder, time to second guess every move he had made. For all his bravado and outward self-assuredness, he was terrified of dying, of losing that final bit of control.

He pushed back the creeping negativity and forced himself to focus on what he needed to do. He had two thousand miles ahead of him, and it would take every bit of physical ability he had within him. Flying was arduous; the wind pounded the body like a hundred fists, the cold numbed the fingers and feet, and maintaining proper heading while controlling speed was a constant chore.

He needed to be careful to limit his visibility as he was sure all aircraft channels were being monitored. Authorities would laugh at any report of a flying man, but the shot callers, those who wanted his head, would mobilize and be on him with more assets than he could shake if they heard the report.

As he drifted off to sleep, he let the sounds of the prairie at night take him home. He went back to summer afternoons by the pool with a cold beer and the smell of Tracy's coconut suntan lotion that glistened like tiny jewels on the back of her legs as she lay in the chaise lounge beside him, neither one of them talking, just enjoying the sun and each other's company. They had been content in the knowledge that they had won, found each other in a world where the house always wins. They had beaten the odds and had life by the balls. For a while it really seemed like fate had been paying attention to their lives. The money had been solid and the career paths clear, but as everyone knows, all things end, especially the shiny things in life. It's always just a matter of time before the dark sharp edges come out and the bleeding starts. Everyone gets a wound. Some recover. Most don't. Like his hardcore Range Master at Quantico used to say: "Nobody gets off this rock alive, nobody." Fate -what a bitch.

Chapter Twenty- Six

In the entire time Stone Gate had been in operation, this was only the second time that all the individuals responsible for the program had been in one room. Crawford began his presentation by dimming the room lights and starting the Power Point.

"Gentlemen, this is a schematic of the latest power fluctuations currently being addressed. As you can see, the difference between column six and column seven are dramatic. Note the time hack - these calculations were taken at 0600 this morning." None of the ten men in the darkened room said a word. "And on this slide, you can see that we measured the amount of plasma barrier currently in the phasing array. Again, the measured amounts are very thin, dangerously so."

"So what is our contingency? Don't we still have assets down range?" questioned a voice from the dark.

Crawford clicked on the next slide. "Yes we do. This is Commander Jacob Hauser, the original asset sent in on Operation Noble Shadows. A Seal Team Six operator, he trained for this operation for almost a year. As you all know full well, this mission, at least his part of it, has failed. The time waypoints were not met. We have lost all bio data contact and all Mag/Laser triangulations on this individual."

"Is he dead?" questioned another voice from the dark.

Crawford hit the next slide. "We are not sure. All the bio monitoring dropped off from our side during a major power flare. To answer your question, he may very well be alive. We just do not know. "
"This is Sgt Major Campbell, CAG. He is our back up. As you

know, everyone sent through the Continuum has a number two who can be put into the breech in case the primary fails in some way. We have lost all contact with him as well."

"How serious is this containment issue?" another questioned from the dark. "Are we talking shut down?"

Crawford brought up the next slide. "To answer your question, this is our problem. This picture was taken at 0600 this morning in the containment portal. All that bright blue light in the center of the frame is anti-matter. To give you some scale, all the anti-matter currently produced would be less than one hundred thousandth of a micron, the amount that was put in suspension in France's Hadron Collider last year. More simply - if the amount of anti-matter in Hadron was the size of a dime, the amount seen here in this photograph would be the size of a small car."

Crawford brought up the room's lights from his computer. "As you can see, we have some hard decisions to make."

Greg Mason from JTTF spoke up. "What happens if we lose containment? What's the bottom-line effect?"

Crawford thought for a moment. "If the amount of antimatter clears the containment barrier, our world, as we know it, ends. We don't have a scale that could measure that possible damage," he replied, closing his laptop. "I think we are at a critical juncture here."

"What does Shaw say?" questioned Edmond Price from the Defense Intelligence Agency.

Crawford sat back in his chair. A thin humorless grin crossed his face. "His recommendation is that we shut down. Close the Continuum."
Price cleared his throat. "With the information you have, Director, why has this NOT been done considering the risk?

How much more antidotal data do you need?"

"Not that simple, Ed. By turning off all axillary power to the Continuum and closing down the array field, we may cause the portal to collapse completely. We may not get it back. It would end our ability to travel through time. It would be over, all of it."

Howard Stratton from the State Department, the most senior member next to Crawford spoke up. "So we are choosing between possible world annihilation and keeping the program up and running? I think the decision is an easy one. I agree with your man, Shaw. Shut it down."

"I agree," announced Price. "I think we have been taking too much of a risk for too long already. I think we should shut it down. Why is there even a discussion about this, for Christ's sake?"

"Have you forgotten how many lives we have saved with Stone Gate, how many people have benefited from its use? If you recall, we reversed both Presidential assassinations last year, the terrorists' attack in Virginia, and the forth Gulf War, all in the last two years. Millions are alive today because of Stone Gate."

Price thought for a moment. "Small ball when you think of what could happen if we lose control of this thing. Trust me when I say this, I am exceedingly grateful for all the wonderful reversals that we have been able to accomplish with the program so far. But now we have worked ourselves into a situation that could possibly end all life as we know it. I really do not think we have any other choice. I say we shut it down."

Crawford scanned the faces of the men in attendance, trying to read a consensus. "Is this how everyone feels? We have had the ability to change history for two years, which means we now control the world. The human race at large is much more peaceful because of Stone Gate. Most of the terrorists that caused the havoc over the years have been eliminated. Israel has extended its settlement borders and is peaceful, trade imbalances have been renegotiated, and the economy has never been better. Do we really want to end our ability to influence these types of situations?"

Stratton spoke up. "The domestic front was better during the prior administration, but since the current President has been in office, things have gotten far worse. The job is over his head and has been from day one."

"I don't want to get off topic here, folks," announced Price. "But I could give a shit less about some community-organizing President. My concern is for the safety of the human race. The President is insignificant to the big picture, always has been. If we lose control of this thing, there will not be a country to govern. Let's not forget that."

Crawford had known prior to the meeting that shutting Stone Gate down would be the collective response to this new information. It was the expected knee jerk reaction to a problem that he believed could be solved if given time. He had invested far too much in the project for it to shut down. He simply could not allow that to happen.

"Gentlemen, when you appointed me to this position, every one of you stated in an open assembly that I had your trust and confidence in regards to Stone Gate. I believe that I have earned your trust through effective management providing stunning results over these years. What I ask now is for your continued support. If you can't give your direct support, at least give me some time to work on the difficulties we now face."

"How much time?" questioned Price. "According to your

data, we are down to days, maybe hours."

"Maybe," replied Crawford. "However, my team is currently addressing the problem aggressively. I have great confidence that they will be able to implement a solution. I ask that you give me twelve hours before you issue the order to shut down."

Price looked at the other men sitting around the table, who were nodding in agreement. "All right, you have twelve hours. If the problem cannot be fixed in that time, we shut it down immediately."

Crawford checked his watch. "It is now 9:30. By 2200 hours tonight I will have a solution to the energy flux or I will pull the power. Agreed?"

"I hope we are not erring on the side of overconfidence," announced Stratton. "I am more than just a little skeptical that you will be able to get this under control within twelve hours."

Crawford smiled. He had never liked Stratton, considered him a nutless political lackey who had never stuck his neck out for anything in his life, even things he had supposedly believed in. DC was full of them. He had a file two inches thick on the man and would like nothing better than to drop it on him from a great height the minute he got in the way.

As a point of fact, he had real highly "sensitive" material on every man in the room, material that gave him the luxury of time when he needed it and in most cases the benefit of the doubt in meetings like this. All men of great power have secrets. He had made it his mission to uncover them.

"I have complete confidence, Mister Stratton," replied Crawford flatly. "Gentlemen, that's all I have for now. If you'll excuse me, I have a program to save. As per SOP, all of your phones and electronic devices may be picked up outside the SCIF. The security officer will assist you as you leave. Thank You."

As he left the building, he was glad that he didn't have to play any of the chips he held. In political matters, it was fear that fueled the machine. It kept everyone doing what he or she needed to do. DC politics was a blood sport. With the stakes so high with regards to Stone Gate, only the real meat eaters would survive to call the shots.

As far as the twelve-hour limit that had been put on him, he had no intention of standing by it. Stone Gate would never be shut down. If the neutered shot callers didn't like it, they would have to deal with the shit storm he could dish out. Yeah, fear was a good thing.

Chapter Twenty- Seven

Hauser checked his watch as the Hanover City Limit sign slowly rolled by the train compartment window. It was one thirty in the afternoon and Hanover would be the last stop before getting into Breman. He knew he was a solid sixty miles away from his destination but knew he couldn't ride into the Breman station with a dead body in his compartment. He would have to get off and find other transportation.

He was already standing on his car's lower steps ready to get off when the train eased into the Hanover station. The platform was full of German soldiers and German police checking identification cards and travel documents. Realizing he would need to be very careful, he hopped off before the train had even come to a complete stop and headed directly into the station house. He quickly checked his steps, forcing himself to slow the pace. Knowing that body language could give him away, he worked to appear nonchalant as he walked through the busy station.

He was sure that he would be stopped leaving the station, so he needed to take a moment to look at his documents and collect himself. He headed towards the bathroom trying to blend in with the hustle and bustle of the crowd. He found an empty stall in the bathroom, one farthest from the entrance, and fought the urge to vomit as he closed the stall door behind him.

He was sweating profusely. He could almost hear his heart pounding. He was losing it, gripped in a full-blown panic attack. *Jesus, what is wrong with me* he thought sitting down on the commode. He had been on countless operations in the past where stress had been just as intense, just as oppressive, but he had not experienced this level of nearly debilitating fear before. He clenched his fists and worked at drawing calm deep breaths. "Get control," he whispered out loud. "Get control."

For what seemed like ten minutes he sat in the stall and slowly brought his breathing and heart rate under control. For what he had to do next, he would have to be as cool and calm as possible. Any overt excitability or visible stress could get him arrested or killed on the spot. The German police were barely civil to uniformed soldiers and were heavy-handed and notoriously rough with civilians. To get through the station alive he would need to pull off the best acting job of his life.

Hauser knew that the identification papers he carried would only work in a limited capacity. The travel document stamped by the travel authority in Munich was now outdated. Any real investigation as to who he was and what he was doing in Hanover would not pass close scrutiny. He needed a distraction, something that would make any prolonged contact with him distasteful if not downright repulsive. *It might work*, he thought stepping out of the stall. *All I need now is an un-flushed toilet full of shit.* Thankfully the large restroom was empty as he checked several commodes, finally finding what he needed.

Stepping into the stall, Hauser hesitated before dipping his hand into the foul smelling remains of someone else's meal. *Get tough* he told himself slowly putting his hand into the cold brown water. *It's only shit. It can't kill you.* The foul smelling mass oozed through his fingers as he rubbed the shit on both hands and then the front of his overcoat, the smell making him wretch uncontrollably.

He vomited on the floor missing the commode completely before staggering out of the stall. "Vos Is Loss," shouted someone from the restroom entrance. He was still trying to compose himself when he looked up and to his shock saw two

German police officers in pristine uniform standing just six feet away with a look of such disdain on their faces that it made him chuckle in spite of his situation.

The officers wanted nothing to do with this foul encrusted civilian and held their noses shouting for him to "Get out, Get out now". One of the men kicked him in the backside as he quickly passed by. The crowd stepped aside like Moses parting the Red Sea as he walked through the busy terminal. *Who would have thought that a shit-covered coat would have been my ticket out of danger,* he thought smiling as he stepped outside the station and headed down the narrow street to town. Amazing.

***

Startled from sleep, Clark sat upright trying to focus in on his surroundings. A second odd thudding sound had him throwing off blankets and ripping out of the tent, his heart pounding nearly out of his chest. He laughed to see the source of the sounds. Twenty yards away, three Black Range cows, chewing large mouthfuls of sweet grass, stared at him impassively. By the looks of several fresh cow patties, his visitors had been checking his camp out for a while, a disconcerting fact considering he had slept right through the noise. Anyone could have walked up on him and he would have never heard it.

He sat down at the mouth of the tent, trying to remember a time when he had slept so soundly. He pulled on a shirt and checked his watch, surprised to see that it was already 9:30. He had slept over twelve hours. Overhead the sky was slightly overcast and the air held the smell of rain. The thought of flying through freezing rain held little appeal as he looked out over the rolling hills. Having to land cold and wet along the way before reaching the next waypoint was a proposition he really did not want to explore.

Looking at his tent, he was confident that it would shed water. I have enough food and bottled water to last weeks, so what is the hurry? He pulled on his jacket and stood, scanning the area for firewood. "Coffee," he said to the cows watching him intently. Fire equals coffee.

Clark knew he had seen a Folgers can in the cache the night before. Yep, that was the next order of business. The whole world always looked better after a cup coffee. Besides, lying low for another day would give him a chance to go over Robashaw's notebook and plot the next leg of his travel in better detail. At least that's what he told himself. In reality he was still ragged and sore from the previous flight. All he really wanted to do was have a cup of hot coffee, get back in the tent, and sleep a few more hours. He was safe, he was dry, and for right now that was enough.

Chapter Twenty-Eight

"I need for you to tell me what this means or what you think it means," stated Shaw rotating his laptop on the table.

Philip Crane, one of five quantum physics experts assigned to Stone Gate, looked at the screen as he smoked a pipe. "When did this occur?" he asked looking up.

Shaw checked his watch. "Seventeen minutes ago. I was watching the portal monitors when this reading came through."

Crane sat back in his chair. "There has to be a mistake, some anomaly in the instruments that we are just not finding. There has to be."

"Everything checks out, Phil. I've gone over this data three times now, and it's all correct. We are seeing something new here."

Crane checked the computer again. "Okay, but before I throw cold water on the theory I think you are leaning towards, why don't you tell me what you think this means."

"Last year, just after we reversed the second assassination on the President, Martin Hall out of Caltech published that very interesting paper on Multiverse time slips. Remember?"

Crane nodded. "Yes, I remember. Way too many variables for my taste."

"Well, according to this electron count, his theory has some validity."
"Ah, I am not sure you're on solid ground with that,

Hammond. Remember the Continuum has always registered more as a fluid energy anomaly, not a static one. That is why it has been so difficult to regulate the energy needs for transport."

Shaw smiled. "Which goes back to my point of Halls' multiverse theory. How else do you explain all of the power readings suddenly dropping back to normal?"

Crane thought for a moment as a heavy cloud of cherry scented smoke drifted over his head. "Okay, let's say you're right. Then what are we dealing with now?"

Shaw closed the laptop. "First, it means that we no longer have a potential world-ending event building in the containment array. Secondly, we may have opened an additional Continuum, one in a parallel universe or as Hall wrote, a "*Multiverse reality*"- a functional time slip.

"And you think the nearly catastrophic energy overload and erratic proton flux we were experiencing somehow broke through a barrier exposing this multiverse reality?"

Shaw nodded. "That is exactly what I think, Phil. The massive amount of proton flux and the dark matter input worked like an internal explosion on the Continuum side exposing a different dimensional path, a split in dimensional stasis. It depressurized itself like opening all the windows in a house during a tornado."

"You do know that's a myth don't you, Hammond? The volume of air displaced by opening all the windows in the house is not enough to match the vacuum created by a tornado. Your roof still ends up in Nebraska along with all of your furniture."
Shaw nodded smiling. "Okay, okay, bad example, but my analogy paints a pretty good example of what we are now

looking at. How else would you explain this data?"

"I would say that our energy protocols were sound and all of our system redundancies worked like they were supposed to. We dodged a very big bullet," replied Crane slowly relighting his pipe. "But, I would add that your theory, which is still more speculation than fact, is interesting and deserves further study."

Shaw laughed while punching in Crawford's cell phone number. "Sir, I think we are okay. I can have the data for you within the hour if you like."

Across town, Crawford closed the door to his office, sat on the edge of the desk, and breathed a sigh of relief. "Very good, Doctor Shaw, I will be over tomorrow morning for the briefing at eight o'clock. Please have all the information available. I will need to back-brief the committee later in the day."

"Yes, sir," replied Shaw. "We are going over the final numbers now."

"Thank you, Shaw," replied Crawford disconnecting the call. "Jesus," he whispered. *Stone Gate is still alive.*

*****

Walking down the cobble stone streets on his way into the city, Hauser looked for a place to clean up. He wanted to start writing everything down, but first he needed to get something to eat. Then he would find a quiet room where he could consider his next move before making a run for the coast.

As he crossed the large stone bridge he could see the familiar long red and black Nazi banners hanging from the front of several buildings in the downtown area. From the distance it looked as though the buildings were bleeding a steady stream onto the street. Two teenage girls dressed in green and white school uniforms walked by pushing bicycles, smiling and talking. As they drew near they made faces of disgust. He smiled to himself watching their reaction. His diversion was still working.

Three blocks later he spotted the large blue *Lancer Inn* sign hanging on the front of one of the buildings. It would be as good a place as any to lay low for now. He didn't think he would be able to stand the smell of himself much longer. Wearing other peoples' shit had worn off long ago.

Two miles away, back at the train station, the train steward gently knocked on the door of compartment twenty-six. "Hello, gentlemen, we are leaving the station. Hello." He opened the door slightly and spotted what looked to be a German soldier lying on his back under a blanket. The smell of alcohol hung heavy in the room. He was just about to close the door not wanting to wake the man when the train suddenly jolted forward and the soldier's arm flopped out from under the blanket.

For a moment he stood staring at the man, instinctively understanding what he was seeing. The train was now picking up speed as he crept into the compartment. "Hello, sir" he said softly, gently pulling the blanket off the man's face. He touched the side of the soldier's neck and then stepped back as if an electrical shock had nipped his fingers. The body was as cold as a stone. The dead had been found.

Chapter Twenty-Nine

Two days after the rain started the storm that had blown into northern Idaho from the west ended, leaving the sweet grass and trees surrounding Clark's camp heavy with moisture. While waiting for the storm to pass, Clark had rested in the small tent studying Robashaw's notebook, getting a far deeper understanding of just what Robashaw had been doing all those years crisscrossing the United States with the Medallions. In several passages he seemed well aware of the fact that people in power were after him. In one of the entries he noted that he had been able to slip on the Silver Medal just before a group of foreign-speaking men arrived at his campsite in western Ohio. They had been tracking him, and he had evaded capture by only minutes. That had been a year ago.

As Clark read through the pages, he began to pick up a deep and growing paranoia in the writing, plainly seeing a man desperate to hang onto the power he controlled with the Medallions yet terrified of being caught without them. Over the three and a half year run, Robashaw's emotional state appeared to deteriorate to the point that he was functioning only at a survival level, stealing the supplies he needed to stay alive and then moving on to another safe campsite. There didn't appear to be any objective related to the constant movement, no end-plan or goal. It was as if the Medallions had been driving him on without reason. He just kept moving. He had broken off all contact with family and friends and had stopped using credit cards or any other form of identification. He had stopped driving, stopped using mass transit of any kind, which in itself had made it almost impossible to track him. There simply hadn't been a paper trail to follow. He went where he wanted when he wanted, took what he needed, and then moved on, all under the cloak of invisibility and unassisted flight - an incredible way to live.

In the short time that he had had them, Clark had begun to feel the growing seductive power of the Medallions, the feeling of being accountable to no one or anything. There would be no messy consequences for bad behavior if one chose to follow that path. There would be no legal repercussions for breaking the law as there were no viable laws while the Medals hung around your neck. You could influence, steal, and terrify at will. When he thought about it, why would anyone not want that kind of power, that limitless freedom to do whatever you wanted.

Looking out his tent on the growing sunshine of the day, he was beginning to have a spiritual insight, the ability to see the irony of choice the Medals now provided. Using them, he could have any material possession he wanted, yet possessions became unimportant when you had the Medallions. If he restricted his travel by living in one place, he metaphorically caged himself into a box of his own making, taking away the exhilarating freedom he now felt.

The Medallions stripped away all connections to the manmade world, all the physical and emotional chains he had forged in his life. The big question that was looming larger in his mind by the hour was what real purpose did the Medals hold? Why were they here? The question vanished as the sound of a helicopter thudded away in the distance.

"Shit," he said scrambling out of the tent. He looked up just as the dark Blue Bell Ranger flew by close enough for him to see the faces of the pilot and copilot. As if the chopper had been tethered to a wire, it stopped its wide arch, swinging the tail section around less than sixty yards away.

Clark watched as a dark silhouette shouldering a rifle leaned out on the skid. He just had time to dive into the tent as several rounds snapped by sending large divots of wet turf into the air. He grabbed the Silver Medallion and his backpack and, before rolling back out of the tent, draped the chain around his neck making him invisible. A split second later the tent was shredded by a long burst of automatic weapon's fire. Clark trotted a short distance away and watched as the helicopter landed and three heavily armed men trotted towards the tent firing their weapons as they advanced. It was amazing how much firepower they were pouring into the camp; evidently they were not taking any chances.

"Check the tent or what's left of it!" shouted Frost reloading his MP5. "There is no way he got out of that."

One of the men jerked the shredded tent off the ground. "Ah, sir, he's not here."

Frost stood in disbelief as the men flipped the bullet riddled blankets into the air. "You have got to be shitting me!" shouted Frost looking around the small clearing. "I had my eyes on that tent the entire time. There is no way he got out of there, no way."

Clark eased back a few feet under the heavy bows of a large pine tree that was just on the edge of the clearing. He felt the nearly overpowering need to hide but did not want to miss a second of their amazement and angry confusion. It was hilarious watching the men storm around the campsite getting more freaked out by the minute. It was all he could do to keep from walking over to Frost and giving him a Wet Willie.

The power he felt standing just yards away from the men who had just tried to kill him was incredible. These were hard-core professionals who were the best in the world with their skill-set, men who were as comfortable firing weapons as they were eating. He had to quickly remind himself just how dangerous things really were, no matter how much enjoyment he was getting out of their confusion.

Frost and his team were now going through the cache pit, examining the supplies and taking pictures with their camera phones. "Sir, this is Frost. Ah, we missed him again. I really can't explain it."

Standing in his office, Pryor gripped the phone. "I am really getting tired of your failure in this operation, Agent Frost. How hard can it be to kill one man, Mister? Tell me that."

Frost slung his weapon and kicked a small can of condensed milk back into the cache pit. "Sir, I have personally seen this individual FLY."

"Excuse me?"

"Fly, I have seen this guy fly, unassisted flight, fifty yards in front of the chopper. I shit you not - this guy was flying. And now here we had him dead to rights, saw him on the goddamn ground. He dove into a tent. We opened up, and he was gone, like some kind of magic trick."

"What tent? Where?" asked Pryor. "Listen, Frost, put one of your team members on. You're obviously losing it."

Frost handed the cell phone to one of the SEAL snipers who was standing near by. "He wants to talk to you."

"Me?"

"Just take the damn phone. It's Deputy Director Pryor."

"'Yes, sir. How can I help you sir?" announced the SEAL.

"Who am I speaking to?" questioned Pryor sitting down behind his desk.

"Sir, this is Senior Chief Dixon."

"Okay, Chief Dixon, I need you to tell me what in the hell is going on out there. What are you people doing? This should have been over three days ago."

"Yes, Sir," replied Dixon walking away. "Ah, it's really kind of hard to explain. I mean, all of us saw this guy flying. It was pretty incredible. And ten minutes ago we spotted Clark on the ground, just like Mister Frost said. We had a clear target, opened up with everything we had, and he disappeared."

"Disappeared?"

"Yes, Sir - vanished. Would not have believed it if I hadn't seen it myself, Sir. I've spent seven tours in Afghanistan, saw a lot of crazy shit, but I have never seen anything like this. Never."

Pryor thought for a moment. "All right, put Frost back on."

Frost took the phone. "Frost here."

"Pull your team, Agent. Head back to Spokane. This guy has been staying in contact with me. Hopefully he will call again, and we can find out what we are dealing with."

"Yes, Sir. We'll be standing by."

Pryor disconnected the phone and then threw it hard against the wall. "Son of a bitch!" he shouted. How in the hell was Clark doing this – vanishing, flying? Christ. He now knew he was going to have to see Crawford and let him know what was going on in Idaho, a visit he was not looking forward to.

Clark watched as the men slowly walked back to the chopper

that was spinning up forty yards away. He had only heard one side of the conversation, but judging the body language of the group, they had been pulled off the operation. Right now Pryor was probably on his way to talk to his superior about what had happened. It would really be an interesting meeting to see. How was he going to explain this? How could anyone explain this for that matter?

By the time the chopper lifted off, Clark was already punching Pryor's number in on his disposal phone. This was going to be fun.

Chapter Thirty

Crawford had been going over the latest data on the power surges when Shaw walked back into his office. He had been watching the ionized plasma levels in the array drop dramatically, something totally unexpected. Crawford set the data sheets on Shaw's desk. "So, you think we are out of the woods on this, and if we are, how do you explain it? I have a briefing in one hour."

Shaw sat down behind his desk while opening his laptop. "Well, Sir, the way we have this figured and this is only a preliminary theory mind you, we think the massive amount of proton and ionized plasma pressure, an amount that would come close to equaling the gravitational pull of a small star, caused a second fissure or time slip to open up within a micron of the original Continuum -a second doorway."

"Jesus Christ," whispered Crawford.

"Yes, Sir, quite an incredible event. It caught us all by surprise. We are still not sure what it means other than we may now have a small glimpse into another dimensional split, much like being in a dark room and looking through a tiny crack in the door with bright light on the other side."

Crawford was stunned by the information. A second Continuum? If true, the possibilities were staggering. "Are we able to physically access it?"

Shaw turned his laptop around. "Well, Sir, that is an interesting question. If you look here, you can see the second anomaly plasma spray on the latest electron reflector scan."

"I'm not sure what I am looking at here," replied Crawford.

Shaw pointed to the thin orange line next to the graph scan. "This orange line indicates where the anomaly is currently located within the hemisphere grid; the energy activity is producing this high amount of protons. Incredible."

Crawford shook his head. "Well, okay. What does this mean, Doctor? Layman's terms please?"

Shaw sat back in his chair. "The easiest way I can explain it is that the pressure build up generated from the original Continuum, for some still unknown reason, expelled nearly three quarters of its mass. The incredible Dark Matter release event created a seam within the multi-dimensional fan. Bottom line, it opened a door to a possible fourth dimension - uncharted ground to say the least."

Crawford thought for a moment. "All right, when will we be able to access it?"

Shaw smiled incredulously. "Sir, this is a discovery that is going to take years to analyze. The data we currently have will take months to sort out. I would need three maybe four times the amount of staff just to start getting any kind of workable information from this."

Crawford nodded. "Okay, I will get you the people you need. I want a full court press on this second anomaly, Doctor. Also, what does this mean for our current operation? Where do we stand?"

"Well strangely enough, Sir, all of our bio settings and phase array vectors defaulted to the original headings and power feeds after the surge."

"Which means?"

"Which means, that if any of our Noble Shadows' assets are still alive and are still in possession of a working return activator, they can come home."

"So, all our assets downrange have to do is activate the Phase Array device to return. Correct?"

"Correct."

Crawford nodded. "All right then, let's hope they are alive and will at least try to get back. Let me know the minute you get a ping or a return. I'll need to see them right away."

"Yes, Sir, I will contact you. Sir, you do understand that we really don't know much about this new discovery. We are way behind on the information curve."

Crawford stood up and pulled on his overcoat. "Continue with your work, Doctor Shaw. I will get you the people you need. Don't lose your focus. I am going to need some answers fairly quickly."

To Shaw, it was amazing how Crawford could admonish and threaten both at the same time. Even his compliments carried a subtle sharp edge. "Yes, Sir. We should have some more in-depth information in a day or so." The second he said it, he immediately regretted the statement.

Crawford stopped just before leaving the office. "That soon?" he said turning around. "Humm, very well, Doctor. I will be anticipating your call." He left the room, seeming to take all the oxygen with him.

Shaw sat back in his chair feeling as if a thousand pounds had just been piled on his shoulders. "Shit," he whispered. *This bush-league need for approval and over-promising will some day get me killed*, he thought glancing back at the computer screen.

He knew that to Crawford he was just a number, a person filling a slot within a mission that would not stop or even slow down, no matter who stumbled or fell along the way. The only thing he was sure of when working with Director Crawford was that nothing was for sure. Nothing.

***

It was well after three in the afternoon by the time Hauser checked into the Lancer Inn, washed the shit out of overcoat, and took a hot bath to get rid of the rest of the filth he had collected while walking around for the last couple of hours. He now sat at the small desk by his room's window that overlooked the busy street. Hanover appeared to be a bustling town; a steady stream of cars, busses and trucks rolled by on the avenue below.

He opened the window a crack, letting in the cold fresh air tinged with the smell of muddy snow. He pulled out the paper and pens from the small backpack trying to think of where to start. Most importantly, he was still trying to figure out who he would be sending the information to. His parents had not met yet in 1939. His father was still a boy, maybe eight or nine years old. His mother was around five. The only solid address he had for any of his relatives was in Saint Joseph, Michigan. His grandparents had a home a stone's throw from Lake Michigan, a home that had been in the family for generations. He had been there many times as a kid during summer vacations, days filled with swimming in the always cold lake water and fishing in the deep and slow moving Saint Joseph River with his Grandfather, a stoic man who kept conversation to a minimum and his emotions even closer. He had been a product of the Great Depression, a trauma that had marked him deeply for life.

The address was a short rhyme that he had never forgotten, "Seven two seven heaven." His grandparents lived at 727 Haven Street, Saint Joseph, Michigan. As he addressed the large brown envelope, he was surprised that he still remembered it. He wrote down his grandmother's name, knowing that she was the one that always went to the post office. His grandfather had always found mail to be a nuisance and had little to do with it. Even as a kid he remembered that his grandfather had spent most of his time fishing the Saint Joseph River.

He took all six orange and white Nazi stamps he had bought out of the stationary box and stuck them in a neat row on the envelope. He would give anything to see his grandmother's face when a large envelope with Nazi stamps arrived in her box, especially from a grandson who hadn't even been born yet.

As he began to write, he knew it was a long shot that the envelope would even be delivered much less read. But as he filled up page after page of information about who he was and where he was, the better he felt. He wrote about becoming a SEAL, about his nine tours in Iraq and Afghanistan, wars eighty years in their future. He wrote about his divorce and how losing his wife had nearly cut him in half. He told of the incredible opportunity and honor when selected for a special government project called Stone Gate and the Noble Shadows mission in particular. He wrote of how time travel had been discovered and the manipulation of world events had become routine. He then wrote about how he was stuck in 1939, desperately trying to get back to his country before World War Two started for the United States. Jesus, he thought, Pearl Harbor had not even happened yet. Maybe he should put that in even though he felt sure she would not believe it.

He wrote for two hours, telling her everything that had

happened from the killing of the German police officer and soldier on the train to the unexpected death of Campbell, his teammate. He realized that the room was getting dark as he looked up from his writing, the late November sun a faded purple haze on the horizon. The streetlights were coming on down below, casting long shadows on the wet pavement.

He sat back in his chair and turned on the desk lamp feeling an odd yet pleasant release of emotion. He had told her everything, chronicled every event that had led him to this point. He wasn't religious, but this had to be how people felt after confession, unburdened of great and terrible secrets, having given the emotional load and hard truth over for others to carry. For the first time in days, he felt at peace as he carefully folded the multipage letter and slid it into the envelope. Other than leaving a written account of what had happened to him, the letter would serve no real purpose, he thought, pushing back his chair. And then again, if God was paying attention, He might just step in and do something, anything.

With the thought of possible divine intervention hanging heavy in his mind, he pulled on his still damp overcoat and stuck both 40-caliber pistols in the bottom of his pockets. He needed something to eat and the café just down the street looked decent. Before leaving the room he stuffed the envelope under his mattress. He locked the door while stepping into the dimly lit hallway.

He nodded to the dozing desk clerk on his way out and stepped out into the early evening cold, immediately feeling just how damp his overcoat still was. Fortunately, he only had to walk a block, time enough to think more about what God could do and of how his grandmother might react to the letter. Both were forces of nature. Both he desperately needed to reach. He had long since stopped counting on luck, resigned himself to the sharp edges of cause and effect. It was a hard way to live if you were counting on a miracle, very hard indeed.

Chapter Thirty-One

Pryor was nursing a second scotch and soda when his cell phone buzzed on the bar. He had stopped at Hales Grill after getting a call from Clark three hours ago taunting him with the fact that he was still alive somewhere in Idaho. Pryor had immediately notified Crawford with the news and had been summoned to his office to properly explain himself. He thought back to that meeting.

After reading the AAR (After Action Report) from Pryor's team in Idaho, Crawford sat back in his chair, showing no signs of emotion. To Pryor, the lack of any outward response to this outlandish report of Agent Clark flying and disappearing was downright unnerving. Any "normal" person reading the report would have been outwardly amazed if not visibly skeptical.

"Sir, what are your instructions?"

Crawford thought for a moment, his expression flat. "How many times has Clark escaped capture?" he asked finally.

"Three times, three times when we were sure he was caught. I honestly believe that he is doing something to evade capture, something that we have never seen before."

"Have there been any press releases about this anywhere?"

"No, Sir. Although that has been a verbal threat from Clark from the beginning, nothing has been put out."

"And his demands are to move through the Continuum? That's what he wants in exchange for these objects that give him his extraordinary ability?"
"Yes, Sir, that's correct."

"All right, Mike, thank you for the information. I will get back to you before close of business today. Just stand by your phone. I need to make some calls."

Pryor left Crawford's office feeling like a man who had just escaped the gallows. Now two drinks into his "Standing- by" his cell phone was buzzing. "Yes Sir."

"I am rescinding the elimination order on Clark," announced Crawford as calmly as if he were ordering a meal. "Arrange a meeting. We need to see what we are dealing with before any other action is taken. Pull your teams off. Are we clear?"

"Yes, Sir," replied Pryor breathing a silent sigh of relief. "I will set it up. I will…"

Before he could say anything else, Crawford disconnected the call from his end, a habit that Pryor found infuriating. It was a classic non-verbal, passive aggressive control technique that Crawford had used since Pryor had known him. It was also a clear indication of what Crawford really thought of him, which was very little by his estimate.

"Asshole," he whispered under his breath while punching END on his phone. He motioned to the bartender. "Hit me again, Steve."

The bartender poured the drink and set it on a coaster. "Tough day, huh? "

Pryor took a sip shaking his head. "You have no idea, my friend. No idea."

***

Sixteen hundred miles to the east, Clark was doing his best to stay on a heading. He had been flying for two days now, dodging rainstorms, high winds and really cold temperatures at anything above four thousand feet. If all went according to plan, he would find his next waypoint just on the west side Lincoln, Nebraska. According to his GPS, he was now within fifteen miles of where he needed to land.

As he dropped altitude through the gray overcast sky, he could feel a slight rise in temperature. Even three degrees was a welcomed respite from the numbing cold. How did a man of Robashaw's age do this, he thought still descending? He pulled his knees in tight while arching his back coming to a dead stop sixty feet off the ground. God it felt good to stop, he thought gently settling to the ground. He had landed in a small clearing surrounded by old growth trees within sight of a slow moving stream, its banks choked with reeds and cattails.

He sat down on the damp ground trying to rub the warmth back into his thighs as a voice from the weeds ten yards away spoke up. "Holy shit!"

Stunned, Clark stood up, trying to see where the voice had come from. He quickly peeled off his frosted-over goggles and peered into the thick brush. "Who's there?" he shouted, debating if he should just take off running. He was sure he could clear the trees and be gone in seconds.

A man in his late sixties stepped out of the weeds. To Clark, his appearance alone was not what drew his attention, but the long barreled shotgun cradled in his arms. 'Thought I had seen everything there was to see. Now you showed up."

Clark took a step back still not sure of his next move. On closer inspection he could see that the man was wearing a camouflaged hunting vest and knee high rubber boots. "I, ah , I, really don't know what say," stammered Clark, backing up a step.

The man stepped forward lowering the shotgun. "Well, maybe you can tell me how you can fly. That might be a good place to start."

"Really not sure I owe you an explanation, Sir."

"Well, mister, I think you do. My name is Bud Allen and I own this property." He brought the shotgun up. "And you're trespassing on my pheasant grounds."

Clark slowly raised his hands. "Listen, Mister Allen, I don't want any trouble. If you just give me a minute, I will be out of here and we can forget this meeting ever happened, okay?"

Allen took another step forward. "Listen I am not trying to be a hard ass about this, I'm really not, but you have to give me some information on what I just saw. Goddamn, I just watched you fly, so who are you and what the hell is going on?" The bird hunter stepped closer, his face clouded with barely-controlled fear.

Clark lowered his hands, forcing himself to take a relaxed posture. He unstrapped his helmet and slipped his backpack off his shoulders. "How much time do you have?" he asked.

The look of fear turned to one of confusion. "What are you talking about?"

"It's a long story. How much time do you have?"

"Shit, I got all day," he said, lowering the shotgun to his side, "That was the damn-dest thing I have ever seen. Who are you? You from around here?"
Clark extended his hand. "Name is Dave Clark, Mister Allen, FBI."

Allen shook hands, his mouth open as if he was trying to gulp air. "Holy shit, no kidding? Man, I knew this had to be some kind of government shit."

"Pretty good guess, Mister Allen. I, ah,...."

"You can call me Bud, Agent Clark," interrupted Allen smiling. "Everybody around here calls me Bud."

"Okay, Bud, well as I said, I am with the FBI, and we are doing some investi..."

"Ah, you wouldn't have some identification on you, would ya?" interrupted Allen stepping closer. "I think I would feel better knowing you were the real thing. No offense."

Clark had had enough. "Shit," he said snatching the shotgun out of the man's hands. "Goddamnit, you just have to keep pushing huh?" he shouted racking the slide back on the gun, ejecting the round. He then unscrewed the mag tube cap and pulled the barrel off the stock and receiver.

"Jesus, Mister, I, I, I'm sorry. Don't kill me. I...I...I got grand kids."

Clark tossed the two pieces of the shotgun into the weeds and the cap screw over his shoulder. "Relax, pal, nobody is going to kill anyone. I just gotta get warmed up and get something to eat. I'm cold. It's getting dark and having trouble with you is the last thing I need. Trust me on that one, and put your hands down for Christ's sake."

Allen seemed to relax. "Ah, good, fine," he replied, breathing a sigh of relief. "Is there anything I can do?"

Clark thought for a moment while scratching his scalp. "You know, Bud, maybe there is. You have a phone?"

Chapter Thirty-Two

By eight o'clock the next morning Hauser was already up and having his second cup of coffee at the café he had eaten supper at the night before. The waiter had brought him eggs, sliced tomatoes and toast, which he took his time with while trying to decipher the Denmark shipping schedule he had picked up at the kiosk near the hotel. If he was reading the paper right, a passenger ship called the Astor Clipper would be leaving the Port of Hamburg tomorrow at midnight, a solid seventy-five miles from Hanover.

The ship was registered under the flag of Denmark, which meant German citizens were able to book passage. It was bound for New York, perfect for what he wanted to do. Stuffing the schedule into his coat pocket, he sipped the last of the strong coffee and headed out the door. The wind had picked up and the temperature had dropped, but the sky was a brilliant blue, a good day to travel. He pulled his coat collar tight and made his way down the busy street feeling rested and strong. He knew the train station was crawling with German police, and not having official travel documents would be a major problem. His plan now was to catch a bus or hire a car to take him the seventy-five miles to the port.

Up ahead on the left, he spotted the now familiar blue and white post office sign. A large red, black, and white Swastika flag fluttered out front in the early morning breeze, giving the building a festive yet macabre appearance. No matter how much time he spent around the Nazi flags and banners he never got used to them. He bounded up the short flight of stairs and opened the heavy glass door, the warm pungent smell of a coal stove burning inside washing over him. There were already several people standing in front of the window waiting their turn to mail letters and packages.

He checked his watch and then got in line. He could have just dropped this thick envelope into the out bin by the door and hoped for the best, casting his documentation to fate. But something inside of him needed to personally hand off this message to his Grandmother. He knew the letter was a long shot attempt but he needed to try.

Finally stepping up to the window, the short clerk with glasses greeted him. "Good morning, what can I do for you, Sir?"

Hauser slid the thick stamped envelope under the glass. "I am sending this to the States. Is there enough postage?" he asked in German.

The clerk read the address and nodded slowly. "Of course, Sir. You have more than enough postage to get it there. May I ask who the recipient is?"

Hauser was caught off guard by the question, not sure if the clerk was acting in an official capacity or just being curious. The hair on the back of his neck was now standing up. "I, ah, it's my aunt, my mother's sister. She loves to read the German papers. I try to send them to her whenever I can."

The clerk smiled and tossed the envelope into a large canvas bin by his side. "You sound like a good nephew. She should have her papers in about three weeks." He leaned close to the glass, a conspiratorial grin crossing his face. "Although I cannot vouch for the American postal service."

Hauser smiled and stepped back from the glass. He had done it, sent a metaphorical flaming arrow of information into the void of time. He nodded to the clerk and turned only to come face to face with two uniformed German police officers. For a second that seemed like an hour, Hauser made eye contact with one of the officers, nodded, and then walked by as the two moved forward in the line.

He stepped outside, willing himself to move slowly, casually. The last thing he needed now was to draw attention to himself. He walked down the steps and headed up the street, slowly getting his heart rate and breathing under control. He crossed the busy avenue and walked another five blocks before he spotted the main road signs that led north out of the city.

As he walked along the road, he thought about Campbell's family. He hadn't known the man long enough to find out if he even had a family. Did he have a wife and kids? Maybe, parents? Hell, everybody had parents. How would the government explain his death to those who cared about him? That was just it; they wouldn't. There would be no explanation, no closure. It would be as if he had never existed, a terrible way to end a life of total dedication and service to the cause. To Hauser, the price and sacrifice he had made to be an operator held no regrets. He would do it all again. But to be forgotten, erased from all collective memory, was something almost too terrible to think about.

He pushed the negative thought from his mind, pulling himself back to the moment and on to the challenge of getting transportation to the coast. He had seventy miles to go and still had no idea how he was going to do it. He shoved his hands deep into his overcoat pockets as a cold gust of winter wind blew by. Not being able to think of any other option, he turned and walked slowly backward holding his thumb out, the already universal sign of hitchhikers.

He walked for an hour before a black four-door sedan went by and then pulled over onto the grass shoulder of the road. Relieved that someone had finally stopped and for a possible chance to get out of the cold, he trotted up to the passenger side door. "Hey, thanks for stop..." Before he could say another word, a man stepped out of the passenger side door and raised a pistol, pressing the barrel hard against Hauser's temple.

"Get in," he commanded, grabbing the front of Hauser's collar, shoving him towards the open door. A second man was now out of the car pushing and kicking him in the back.

"Who are you people?" he shouted, already knowing the answer. They had found him.

"Police. You are under arrest," shouted the man kicking and pushing. "Get in the car."

On purely survival instinct, Hauser gripped the forty-caliber in his pocket and fired three quick rounds through his coat into the chest of the man who was holding a pistol to his head. The rounds punched through the man, blowing out the back window of the car. Stunned, the second man stopped his attack as Hauser spun around and fired two rounds into his face, dropping him into a lifeless heap in the tall grass along the road.

The driver was now out of the car and had managed to fire two panic shots from his pistol over the roof. Both went high and to the right as Hauser spun around, crouched, and fired three rounds through the open rear door, hitting the man in the lower chest and belly. Jolted backward by the impact, he was immediately struck by a passing truck as he fell onto the roadway. In less than twenty seconds three German police officers lay dead. Still in combat mode, Hauser ejected the magazine from his weapon and loaded a fresh one. Cars and trucks were beginning to stop and pull off the road as he closed the two passenger side doors of the sedan and walked around to the driver's side. He slid in behind the wheel, shifted the car into gear, and pulled back onto the roadway, his mind still trying to process what had just happened.

Shit, he thought pounding the wheel, *now what?* In five days he had killed five Germans, five deaths that could cause catastrophic consequences to the future. In his entire pre-jump briefings it had been mandated, commanded not to have any physical contact with the local population. Any interaction could change the course of collective history, something completely out of the Noble Shadows' protocol. As he pushed the sedan to go as fast as it would go, his escape and evasion training began to kick in. He would drive the car a mile farther up the road and ditch it. He would then move on foot, avoiding the main thoroughfares. After this, the roads would be heavily patrolled and checkpoints would be everywhere. The killing of three Gestapo officers would not be taken lightly.

Minutes later he spotted a dirt road that branched off the main roadway to the right. Downshifting, he turned, following the well-worn path. Keeping his speed down, he followed the road a mile and a half as it wound through the pristine German countryside. In another quarter mile the path ended in a tall grassy clearing, surrounded by a large stand of pine trees. A small-dilapidated brick house stood empty nearby, its front door hanging sideways off the hinge.

He turned off the engine and sat quietly collecting himself, thinking about his next move. Looking at the interior of the car he noticed a P40 submachine gun on the passenger side floor with a dark brown leather four-magazine pouch lying beside it. In the back seat were assorted legal papers and what looked to be the remnants of a pastry. A small automatic pistol was lying in the floorboard.

He reached over and picked up the machine gun, having never seen one up close. He was surprised by its heavy weight. He ejected the magazine and pulled back the bolt. A 9mm round flipped through the air, landing in the back seat. "Son of a bitch," he whispered. The weapon was ready to go.

If they had opened up with this at close range, he would have been cut to pieces.

He reloaded the weapon and laid it on the seat beside him, still not sure what he should do next. By now the manhunt would be in full swing. Roadblocks and spot checkpoints would be on all the main roadways. This was not even counting the regular Army's search teams that would be combing the countryside. He looked in the rear view mirror before stepping out of the car, his only company - a noisy murder of crows somewhere in the trees.

Standing in the tall grass listening for any sound of pursuit, he took a mental inventory of what he had: two suppressed forty-caliber pistols with three full mags, a P40 sub gun with five mags, a small 9mm pistol with one mag, one thousand Marks in local currency, assorted identification documents, and the well worn clothes on his back. Not much, he thought buttoning his coat. Pulling his collar tight, he discovered Campbell's small plastic return activator still on a chain around his neck. He hadn't been able to throw it away, subconsciously hoping that someday it might work. He knew it was only a weak hope, but it was better than none.

He slung the weapon over his shoulder, resigned to the grim proposition that he was going to go down swinging. He really had no choice, circumstance and willful decisions had put him in this deserted clearing. As he walked through the tall wet grass his mind began to clear and the slight tremor in his legs caused by adrenalin stopped. He was still up, still moving and still in the game, he told himself. "Stay focused, stay motivated, stay alive." He whispered the mantra several times just as he came to a high rock wall that seemed to run for miles in either direction.

He climbed over and jumped down onto the dark plowed ground on the other side. He had always liked the smell of plowed turf; it reminded him of home, the smell of life, his life back in Montana. Every fall the wheat fields all around Missoula would be plowed under, filling the air with that country smell.

It was tough walking through the big clods of turf; his street shoes carried little traction. But the sky was clear and the air was fresh, a combination that made him smile. This really was beautiful country, he thought looking at the open ground ahead of him. His dad would have loved to see this. Feeling a small pebble work its way into his shoe, he stopped and knelt down just as a sound he had heard a thousand times before snapped by two feet over his head. He dove to the ground as a second rifle round thudded into the turf a foot away off to his right.

They had caught him and now someone with a rifle was trying to finish the job. Son of a bitch, he thought, rolling onto his side to reach the P40. He had been caught out in the open, violating every E and E tactic lesson he had been taught. A third, a fourth, and then a fifth round slammed in, kicking up bits of turf all around him. He was now taking fire from several long guns, probably a squad of regular German Army.

It was hard to tell, but he estimated that the shots were coming from the base of the tree line near his abandoned car. His only chance would be to get back to the rock wall and run diagonally in either direction, using the wall for cover. It was his only chance. Another round thudded in, this time less than an inch from his elbow. Time was up. He had to move.

Scrambling to his feet, he ran crouched as fast as he could, stumbling over the muddy clods. Another round hissed by his ear and then another slammed into the top of his shoulder knocking him backwards and into a seated position on the ground. Stunned, he tried to raise the P40 off his lap as several uniformed Germans climbed on top of the wall. With the last bit of will and strength, he raised the machine gun and pulled the return activator out of his shirt, pulling the trigger and pushing the button at the same time. He never felt the fusillade of rounds that slammed into his body nor the frigid cold and bright blue flash of the Continuum taking him away. Neither sensation mattered now. He was already home.

Chapter Thirty-Three

Clark punched in Pryor's phone number while sitting in Allen's beat up pickup truck watching the sun go down. He was well aware of the possible repercussions of using Allen's cell phone, but he needed a witness to his ability, someone to tell the arriving search team the incredible power he possessed. Hopefully that would be enough to convince Pryor to make a deal. It was a long shot but it was his hope.

Pryor answered on the second ring. "Pryor."

"Hello, Mike. How's the world domination business?"

"Don't have time for small talk, Clark. I was told to make a deal with you. Set up a meeting."

Clark was stunned. "Ah, you know, Mike, I watched your guys machine gun my tent a couple of days ago, so you'll forgive me if I think you're full of shit?"

"Think what you like, asshole. Someone way above my pay grade rescinded the elimination order. No one is chasing you now. The next move is up to you".

Clark thought for a moment while looking over at Allen, who appeared to be fascinated hearing one side of the conversation. "Okay, Mike, just for grins, let's say I believe you. What's the meeting for? What possible benefit would it be for me? You guys have been trying to kill me for a month now. Now all of the sudden we're friends?"

"Listen, Clark I am passing on the information I was told to pass on. No one is looking for you now, and that's the truth. My superiors want to talk, which means you might get your life back. Sounds like a good deal to me."

"What guarantee do I have that this is not a setup, that the minute I show my face one of your long range hitters doesn't puts a .308 through my forehead?"

"Hey, Clark, as far as I'm concerned you're a low life piece of shit, and I would like nothing better than to blow your brains out. You killed a good man in Tonga, and I will not forget that. But what I am telling you about the rescinded elimination order is the truth. I don't have time to fuck around on the phone with you, so if you want a deal, call me back."

Clark was about to reply when the call was ended by Pryor.

"I'll be dammed," whispered Clark out loud. He looked over at Allen. "Hey, Bud, you think I could buy a meal from you? I've got money."

Allen thought for a moment. "You mean go to my house?" he replied, more than a little alarmed. "Jesus, my wife is there. What am I going to tell her? Hell, I still have no idea what's going on myself. And just so you know, I paid three hundred dollars for that shotgun you threw in the weeds."

Clark laughed. "Bud, you're all right. Tell ya what I'm going to do." He set his backpack on his lap and rummaged around inside. "Here's twelve hundred dollars for a new shotgun and another, let's see, five hundred for the meal. Does that make us square?"

With an open mouth, Allen took the money. "You're going to give me seventeen hundred dollars for a three hundred dollar shot gun and a plate of left over pot roast?"

Clark nodded and smiled. "You know, Bud, pot roast sounds real good right now. What do you say?"

Chuckling, Allen started the truck shaking his head. "I'd say this is going to be one hell of a dinner conversation, Mister Clark, one Inez won't soon forget."

***

The medical examiner lifted the eyelid of the body lying on the steel drain table under the bright lights of the exam room. Hauser had tumbled into the phase array from the Continuum three hours earlier, and Shaw had contacted Crawford within minutes. All of Stone Gate's medical pre-jump procedures and post mortem exams were held here at a special classified annex just south of the Bethesda Navel Hospital radiology lab. The windowless building had its own subbasement driveway and twenty-four hour security that manned the parking garage entryway. It had been in operation for two years now and was used exclusively by Stone Gate operations.

To Shaw, it was hard to connect the vibrant, incredibly healthy SEAL he had interviewed, trained, and sent through the Continuum to the dead man that now lay on the table. His skin had a gray sickly tint to it and with the four-day beard growth, he looked like a man who had aged ten years.

Crawford stepped up close to the table. "Besides the obvious, what's your assessment?" he asked looking at the body.

The doctor picked up a long pair of forceps from the small Mayo stand. "Well, as you can see, the cause of death is from a firearm, actually several weapons. The angle of entry suggests that he was in a seated position and was struck here, here, here and four other locations in the upper thigh, scrotum, and left knee. If I didn't know better, it looks like he was killed by a firing squad. The bullet that killed him was this one here, right through the heart." He took the forceps and opened the small blood red hole in the center of Hauser's chest.

Crawford leaned in close to Hauser's face, sniffing. "He smells like, onions," he announced surprised.

The doctor nodded. "I noticed that too. The simplest explanation is that he was shot in a freshly plowed onion field. Naturally all of his clothing was sent to toxicology for analysis, spore and microbiology samples, but I would be willing to bet he was in an onion field just before he died."

"Any preliminary information on where this field could be located?" questioned Shaw.

The doctor tossed the forceps into the big stainless steel sink at the head of the table. "Yes, the preliminary analysis says the soil samples taken from his clothing matched the soil samples indigenous to northern Germany - spot on match actually."

"Do we have any information on ballistics?" questioned Crawford.

The ME walked over to a large metal table where several files had been stacked. "Yeah, let me see here, ah, here it is. I made some notes earlier. All of the wounds were through and though except for the one in the upper thigh and the one that hit him in the upper right shoulder. I was able to extract both slugs, even though the shoulder round had become more fragments than anything else. Did some prelim ballistic cross checking and found out the bullets that killed your man were fired from a Karabiner 98K, Mauser, 7.92x 57, a standard German Infantry rifle used by the regular army throughout the war, a very nasty round to get hit with at any range up to eight hundred meters."
"What's your best guess on range with this?" questioned Crawford looking back at the body.

The ME walked back over to the small instrument tray and

picked up a second pair of long forceps. He bent close to the body and pulled open the large wound at the top of Hauser's shoulder. "This one here was from a longer range, hard to tell, but definitely not as close as the others. And as you can see, it looks as if he was bent down, maybe running into the round when he was hit. The others were fired at close range, maybe fifteen, twenty feet. The large exit wounds on the torso give us a pretty good indication that the rest were fired at close range. Looks like your man hooked it up with a squad of German Infantry."

Crawford walked over, took the files off the table and handed them to Shaw. "All right, Doctor, thank you for your information. Have the body taken over to the incineration facility. There will be no second post mortem report. Have all of the clothing and possessions shipped over to our facility after Toxicology is finished."

"What do you want me to do with the weapons?" questioned the doctor. "We found two forty calibers in his overcoat pockets."

"Two?" replied Shaw surprised. "Hauser was only..."

"That will be fine, Doctor," interrupted Crawford. "Have the weapons cleared, boxed, and shipped over with the rest of Hauser's possessions."

The ME nodded. "Yes, Sir. I will have the tox reports by tomorrow. Is there anything else you need from my side?"

Crawford shook hands with the man. "Thanks again. I think we have everything we need."

On the ride back to Shaw's lab Crawford was on the phone. "Mike, the Hauser asset is back. Deceased. That's correct.

What I need from you is contact DOD. Give them the training accident explanation. Subject was involved in classified endeavors and the remains were non-recoverable. List the South China Sea as the location of the incident. SEALS are in that area quite a bit. Anyway, use standard protocol. Any questions?"

Shaw stared out the window watching the late afternoon DC traffic roll by, the people in the cars oblivious to the drama and sacrifice happening so near.

"You all right, Doctor Shaw?" asked Crawford, putting his phone back in his suit pocket. "I can see that you're troubled."

"I was just thinking about Hauser's parents," replied Shaw.

"What about them?"

"Well, they have lost a son but will never get the closure a burial gives them."

Crawford thought for a moment. "The way you need to look at this is that this is the price we pay for the work we do. Hauser was a tool that was put into service, a very expensive piece of a equipment, but an asset nonetheless. He knew what he was getting into."

Shaw shook his head. "That's a hard way of looking at this, Sir, if you don't mind me saying."

Crawford leaned close. "SEALS die everyday, Shaw. That's part of the job description. Dying for the good of the country is what they do. Hauser is no different, and he died for the greater good."

Even though they were the only two riding in the back of a

large limousine, for Shaw, it was far too small. This was the repulsive mindset at the core of Stone Gate, a dangerous machine feeding on the bones of good men like Hauser, men who had no idea just how expendable they really were.

"You having doubts about our program?" asked Crawford, lighting his pipe.

Shaw shook his head, getting tired of the lie. "No, Sir, it's just that I knew Hauser, spent a lot of time with him during his prep. He was a friend."

Crawford took a long pull on the pipe and then blew a perfect cherry scented smoke ring. "Let me give you some advice, Doctor," he said, looking out the side widow of the car. "You need to pick your friends more carefully. Friendships can be expensive." He looked at Shaw and smiled. "Especially in our business. Understand?"

Shaw held the Director's gaze and nodded. "Yes, Sir, I understand," the words nearly sticking to the roof of his mouth before he said them. He had no illusions about Crawford and his admonishment. The threat was real. For a fleeting moment he thought about smashing his fist over and over into the Director's face. He was sick of all the passive aggression and would have loved to pound out all the pent up rage he felt. But second thoughts are more likely to be sane thoughts, and the satisfaction of the assault would be short lived. He would just have to be happy with the fantasy, a fantasy that was growing more wonderfully terrible by the day.

Chapter Thirty-Four

Clark sat at Bud and Inez Allen's dining room table for three and a half hours eating pot roast and potatoes and telling his story. Once he began talking, the words just spilled out in a flood. From the killing in Tonga to the Vatican, he told them everything about his desperate journey that had brought him to Allen's field. He could see out the large living room window from the dining room and knew that no cars arrived in the driveway, no sound of helicopters thudded away in the distance, realizing that no one was coming. Pryor had been telling the truth; he was no longer a hunted man. If it had been going to happen, he would have been hit by now.

"Would you like some more coffee?" Inez asked smiling.

"No Ma'am, three is my limit. Thank you very much for the wonderful meal. You have both been so kind." He liked Inez, a retired elementary school teacher. In her early seventies, she still carried the gentle elegance of a dedicated teacher of children. As he excused himself from the table he noticed that his confession of events had left both of the Allens in a quiet reflective mood. As Inez cleared the table, Bud sat quietly drinking his coffee trying to digest what he had just heard.

"So you think you're finally in the clear?" he asked after a moment.

Clark nodded while watching out the large front living room window. "Looks like it. Ah, folks, I'm not really sure why I told you my story. But I feel better having told someone about it."

Bud smiled. "That's all right, Dave. I think anybody faced with the kind of drama you have been through this last month or so would have done the same. But I have to be honest, if I hadn't seen you come down in my pasture like you did, I'd of called Sheriff Billings, and they would have locked you up after hearing all that."

Inez sat back down at the table. "What are you going to do now, Dave?"

Clark walked over and picked up his backpack and jacket. "Well, if I can borrow your cell phone again, I think I will go try and make a deal."

Bud took the phone out of his shirt pocket. "Go ahead. If you want to go out on the front porch, we'll understand."

"Thank you, Bud. Ah, I think you both know that people would probably think you're crazy if you repeat what I told you tonight, don't you?"

Bud nodded and smiled. "You can pretty much count on us not mentioning any of this to our friends at church. I like being a deacon and would hate to have my mental stability brought into question."

"We're fine," added Inez. "You go make your call. I think you need this to be over."

Clark smiled as a heavy melancholy swept over him. These were good people, some of the best of the greatest generation. Inez reminded him of his mother, a person who had always followed the straight path of kindness and compassion while carrying a quiet iron will just behind her eyes.

"Thank you, folks. I'll just be on the porch."

He stepped outside of the warm house, instantly feeling the bite in the November air. It was a beautiful night, the clear sky filled with a million icy stars.

Pryor answered on the second ring. "Yeah?"

"Okay," sighed Clark stepping off the porch. "Let's have a meeting. I'm ready to get this over with."

"Sounds good to me."

"You move- you're dead. Drop the phone," commanded a menacing voice from the dark.

Clark stood in stunned silence as no less than ten laser light site dots danced on his chest. As his eyes slowly adjusted to the dark, three silhouetted figures could be seen, the four-barrel night vision goggles giving them the appearance of large dangerous insects as they stepped forward.

One of the men stuck an MP 5 suppressor under Clark's chin. "I'm Agent Frost, Mister Clark. I've been after you for a while now. Seems like you stayed here too long, dipshit. If I didn't know better, I would think you wanted to get caught."

"Your boss is a lying son-of-a-bitch," replied Clark angrily. " I thought we had a deal?"

"Yeah, well, not with me you didn't. On your knees and put your hands on top of your head, or don't. It makes no difference to me. I would prefer to drop you right here and while I am at it, take out ole' Bud and Inez just for the aggravation you caused. It's your move, tough guy."

Not wanting to put the elderly couple in any more danger, he knelt down. He was quickly handcuffed, patted for weapons, and roughly led away into the dark. He did not know where or who had his backpack but the medals were still safely around his neck as he stumbled through the dark. After a short walk, they stopped at the side of a large black suburban where he was quickly shoved into the back seat. Frost slid in beside him. "Lets go," he commanded the driver.

As the car's headlights came on, Clark could see several police units parked in the grass with lights off along with several heavily armed SWAT team members walking back to the cars.

"All this for me?" he asked, feeling as if he was about to throw up.

Frost pulled the goggles off his head and quickly rubbed his scalp. "Hey, pard, why don't you just keep your mouth shut, okay? I was told to bring you in, not engage you in conversation. Got it?"

He pulled out a cell phone and punched in the number. "Yes, Sir, we have the package. No injuries. We'll be on the bird in ten minutes. Yes, Sir. Thank you, Sir."

Clark didn't say a word the rest of the short trip to the open field where a helicopter was spinning up, the red and white landing lights flashing in the dark. He didn't have to say a thing. It was finally over.

A black hood was roughly dropped over his head from behind as someone pulled him out of the suburban. After shoving him into a seat on the waiting chopper, he could feel other individuals quickly getting in beside him. No more than fifteen minutes had elapsed from the time he had been taken out of the Allen's front yard to the moment when the helicopter lifted off.

It seemed like they had only been in the air a few minutes when he felt the chopper start to descend and heard the sound of seatbelts being unbuckled. "Okay, Clark, we're changing transport. Let's go," announced Frost pulling him out of his seat and onto the tarmac. It was impossible to see anything from under the hood, but he could smell the warm jet exhaust of a running aircraft close by. Strong hands moved him up the narrow flight of steps and into the small cabin of the government Gulf Stream.

After Clark had been pushed into a seat and the hood removed, Frost, who was dressed in full tactical gear, bent over him and fastened his seat belt. "Got about a two and half hour flight. If you got to piss - too bad. Just have to hold it," he announced sitting in the seat across the aisle. Minutes later, Clark watched as the lights from the city of Lincoln rolled by under the window.

Clark leaned over. "Hey, Frost, mind if I ask you where we are headed?"

Frost shook his head. "What did I say about keeping your mouth shut, dipshit? You'll know when we get there, okay?"

Clark smiled. "Okay, whatever you say."

Trying to adjust the pinch of the handcuffs on his left wrist, he tried to think of any options left. He had no idea where the backpack that had Robashaw's diary inside was. The only thing they would find would be the money, some spare clothes and the empty blue velvet Crown Royal bag. The Medallions were resting against his skin under his shirt and long johns.

He was surprised that they hadn't discovered them; for all his tactical ability, Frost wasn't much on pat downs. The rest of the flight was spent in quiet reflection. He had long since made his peace and whatever happened when they landed and the doors opened would just be a repeat of things he had already imagined. In his mind, he had died the minute they grabbed him in the dark.

Thirty minutes later he felt the jet begin to descend. Lights along the Potomac slowly came into view on approach into Dulles. DC was a beautiful city at night, a brightly lit jewel that exuded promise of all things great and grand. The monuments and wide avenues were all remnants of a powerful idea that had long since died.

Within minutes the plane touched down and began a long taxi to a section of the airport Clark had not seen before. As the plane began to power down, Clark could see that they had rolled into a massive, brightly lit hanger.

Frost was already on his feet. "This is your last stop, Clark," he announced bending over and releasing his seat belt. He slung the MP 5 machine gun over his shoulder and pulled Clark out of his seat. "Let's go," he said, motioning toward the now open door. Clark squinted under the bright lights of the hanger as he stepped out onto the stairway platform. A plain-clothes security agent was standing by the closed passenger door of a black limousine parked close to the plane below.

Clark was surprised at how difficult it was to walk down the stairs with his hands cuffed behind his back. Several times he thought he would lose his balance on the way down. As they reached the hanger floor, Frost gripped his shoulder keeping him from moving forward. "Hold still, asshole." Clark felt the cuffs come off as the security agent who had been waiting by the car opened the door. "Get in, Clark," Frost commanded, nudging him forward. As he ducked into the back seat of the car, he remained unaware that the real adventure was just about to start.

Chapter Thirty-Five

"Have a seat, Agent Clark," instructed Crawford from the back seat.

Clark ducked inside and sat down. "And you are?"

Crawford smiled. "Ahh, right to the point, an admirable trait in a man. My name is Crawford. I am the wizard behind the curtain."

"You're in charge of Stone Gate?"

Crawford slowly lit his pipe. "My official title is Director of Operations, has been since the program started and its..."

"Why am I here?" interrupted Clark, already tired of the small talk.

Crawford eased back in his seat. "You're here because you said you wanted to make a deal. The very fact that you were able to stay alive when a large number of very dangerous men were trying to take it from you intrigues me."

"What is Stone Gate, Crawford?" Even saying the words caused physical pain.

Crawford thought for a moment. "Stone Gate is a program that oversees time displacement, history manipulation. The one who first started the project in New Mexico was Dr. Taylor. I believe you were at his residence at one time, investigating a missing persons report."

"I saw something in that burned-out basement," announced Clark, pushing through the growing headache. The two-week "reeducation" briefings the government had subjected him to were kicking in. "It was incredible."

Crawford nodded, puffing on his pipe. "Ah yes, what you saw was the Continuum, the portal. Magnificent, don't you agree?"

"It ruined my life," replied Clark feeling as if he was about to vomit. "It took away everything I had - my career, my wife... everything. You said Stone Gate is involved in history manipulation. Are you talking about time travel? Is that what this is all about?"

Crawford tapped his pipe. "High price to pay indeed just for being a witness, I mean your wife and career, that is. I read your file. You were a first class FBI investigator."

"Answer the question, Crawford. Is Stone Gate time travel? Do you have that capability?"

"Yes, we have the capability. But I think you knew that all along, Agent. Wasn't it your demand to use Stone Gate to quote: *"Take a one way ticket to a place of your choosing?"*

"Yeah, I did," replied Clark, trying to think of a way to get the Gold Medal off his neck. "I guess I just wanted you to confirm it. I have a hard time getting my head around the idea that the United States government has that kind of capability, of being in control of limitless power."

"Well," replied Crawford smiling, "we are finding that Stone Gate does have some limitations. It's true that we can revisit relatively small events such as assassinations, terrorist activity, and financial decisions, events that are not hugely catastrophic in an emotional sense. But there seems to be a metaphysical wall that prohibits any change in negative world events."

Clark shook his head in amazement. "So how long has the "*Manipulation*", as you say, been going on?"

Crawford thought for a moment. "Almost two years now, which brings us back around to you, Agent Clark. I think we may be able to use your specialties for our mutual benefit."

"Yeah, how's that? By the looks of things, I'm already dead. Your boys out there are just waiting for the word."

Crawford looked out the window. "Well, you're still alive for the moment, Agent Clark. But I am glad you understand the severity of your situation."

"You know, Crawford, I'm really getting tired of this back and forth. Tell me why I am still above ground?"

Crawford laughed. "Okay, first you tell me how you were able to evade my people while getting off the flight from Australia without being seen, in particular. Mister Pryor gave me the details."

Clark saw his chance. "I was invisible," he said smiling.

"Really?"

"Yeah, really." He reached under his shirt and quickly pulled off the Gold Medallion instantly vanishing. Crawford let out a gasp.

"My God!" he whispered. Clark sat motionless, watching Crawford struggle with what he was not seeing.

"I assume you're still in the car, Agent Clark," announced Crawford. "The doors are locked, and if you don't show yourself, I will tell Agent Frost to machine gun every inch of the interior of this car. I am sure he and his team would be more than willing."

Shit, thought Clark. Crawford still held all the cards. This was not going like he had thought it would. After a moment he slipped the Gold Medallion back over his neck and reappeared. Whatever was going to happen, he wanted it to happen now. He was tired of the game.

"Absolutely incredible," said Crawford leaning closer. "Now I understand. And I assume the medals also give you the ability of unassisted flight?"

Clark nodded. "But you can only use one at a time. Wearing them both negates the power of each."

"My God, the possibilities." Crawford sat back in amazement. "Astonishing!"

"Okay, Crawford, you've seen my cards. I know you can take them away anytime you like. I give up. I'm tired and I want this over."

Crawford collected himself, still amazed by what he had just seen. "Right, well, first, I need to inform you of something. You encountered the Continuum in its most raw form in New Mexico. We have become aware that those of you that did were changed in some way. That puts you in a special category of individuals."

"Changed, changed how?"

"We're not sure, but an emotional and even a cellular connection is made and this change is measurable, definitive. And, after seeing the abilities that the Medallions provide, it is my opinion that your involvement in the next phase of Stone Gate could be very beneficial to the program."

Clark shook his head. "I'm not following you here, Crawford. Why don't you just take the medals and be done with it. I'll go my way and be out of your hair forever. I'm tired of looking over my shoulder."

Crawford leaned forward. "Well, here is the problem, Mister Clark. You see, I actually *need* an investigator for the next phase of the program, someone like you with a strong investigative background, someone concerned with facts and not emotions. In addition, you are someone with a special connection to the anomaly; you're a unique asset. Don't you want your life to have value again?"

Clark shook his head. "You want me to work for Stone Gate, the same program that has been trying to kill me for the last two months?"

Crawford smiled. "You really have no choice. I can take the medals and reinstate the elimination order. You would not make it out of this hanger alive. Even if you did manage to escape, you would be hunted until caught. As you can see, I have unlimited resources at my disposal. You said it yourself. You have nothing left. You would never have a normal life again. I am giving you a chance to have a new life. It's your choice."

Clark let out a deep sigh, knowing that Crawford was right. The second he had been caught in Bud Allen's front yard, the game had been over. He really had no choice. "Okay, what now? How does my life have value again?"

Crawford smiled and pushed the electric window button. "Let's go," he commanded the Agent standing outside the car. "Down to the lab." He pulled the cell phone from his suit pocket and punched in a number. "Doctor Shaw, I will be at the lab in fifteen minutes. I have someone with me you need to meet. Yes, we are on our way. Thank you, Doctor." He disconnected the call and nodded to Clark smiling. "Welcome to Stone Gate, Agent Clark."

Chapter Thirty-Six

It had been a week since Clark had agreed to be a part of the Stone Gate Operation. He had met Doctor Shaw and a number of the staff running and monitoring the Phasing Array Faculty. On first meeting, Clark had been struck by how nonchalant all of the scientists were as they discussed their parts in the Stone Gate program. They all maintained the rehearsed coolness that many professional athletes convey when speaking before the press, a rock solid assuredness that each was the best at what they did. You either dug the vibe or you didn't.

None made apology or questioned the ethics of changing the past. Instead they held an unshakable mindset that they were the guardians of the greater good and that what they were doing was JUST on all accounts.

After that first oddly disconcerting meeting in the lab on the night of his capture, very little had been said about the Medallions still in his possession. That night, after talking briefly with Doctor Shaw, he had been driven to a high-end apartment building in Crystal City and lodged in a plush three-bedroom apartment with all the amenities of a well stocked home.

Since then, his routine had been daily briefings and training at the facility, starting at eight in the morning and ending around six in the evening. Classes on quantum physics, inter-dimensional time travel, and gravitational anomalies were just part of the pre-jump training schedule. Endless blood draws, and cellular level physical exams were conducted. All nine metal tooth fillings were removed and replaced with plastic amalgamates. Treadmill stress tests, EKGs, and bio and brain wave scans were part of the medical workup. His diet was strictly monitored to insure proper body weight and muscle mass. To Clark, it seemed an incredible amount of testing and care were going into his pre jump preparation.

He had been told that he would be going through a second Continuum time slip that had recently been discovered and that very little was known about this new anomaly. All preliminary indications were that it was in line with the gravitational patterns and static energy of the first anomaly. Apart from that information, getting a fix on where or even *when* he would be deposited was still a question up for debate.

He had also been briefed on the failed *Noble Shadows* operation, a jump that had taken the lives of two men and had failed to change the course of World War Two. For Clark, the very idea of trying to change the history of the war was staggering in its scope, a fact that made him more than just a little concerned for his own continued existence.

"And this is the second return device that you will be carrying." announced Shaw handing the device across the table. It was the morning of the tenth day, and for the third time that week Shaw was going over the pre jump protocol and expectations.

Shaw handed Clark what looked like a small black heavy nylon chest pack. "I would prefer you carry the Medallions in this. We are not sure what kind of heat ranges the medallions might draw as you move through the Continuum. I would hate to see them melt a hole through your chest."

Clark smiled. "Yeah, that would be a bad thing."

Shaw walked over to one of the large stainless steel lab tables and picked up a large manila file. "I have been over your next of kin records. It says your ex-wife lives in Albuquerque, New Mexico. Do you want her to be notified in case something happens?"

Clark thought for a moment, not able to stop the melancholy from showing in his face. "No, that's okay. My mom is still alive. Make her my POC. That address in Dayton is still correct."

Shaw nodded and closed the file. "You having second thoughts about this?"

Clark laughed. "Yeah, from the minute I walked in the door. Why, you don't?"

Shaw grinned. "It's my job to be clinical. Learning to be stoic is a mandatory class at MIT. It's a place where personalities go to die. I thought you would have picked up on that by now."

Clark chuckled. "Yeah, I did. You want to see the medals again, Doc?"

Shaw smiled. "Can I? We were instructed not to question you about them."

Clark reached into his collar and pulled on the chains, exposing the Medallions to the bright lights of the lab.

Shaw whistled softly. "My God, those truly are magnificent. I am amazed every time I see them. Incredible."

Clark laid the medals on the table. "Why do you think I have been allowed to keep them? I mean Crawford could have given the order to take them away at any time."

Shaw picked up the Silver Medallion, transfixed by its brilliance. "I guess he figured that being with you was the safest place for them to be. You have them on you 24 -7 and we have you 24..." His voice trailed off, realizing the gaff. "Hey, I didn't mean you were some kind of prisoner or something. I apologize if it came across that way."

"No need to apologize, Doc. I know what I am doing here. Where would I go even if I wanted to leave? What would I do? Can't go back to the FBI or the ex wife. No job and no real prospects. I really don't think I could live a quote "normal life" after all that has happened. I think this jump is a natural extension of the things that have already taken place. Besides, I have always wanted to do something of great value. That's why I joined the FBI in the first place. Maybe this is my chance."

Shaw handed the medal back. "I hope so, Dave. I really do."

***

Three days later, Crawford sent the order that the jump would take place at 2100 hours of the following day. The night before the jump Clark tried to suppress the building anxiety of what was to come. He had been told that the array date set for his jump would be calibrated for two days in the past, hopefully giving him a discernable time reference on the ground. Time jumping into the past was one thing. Time jumping into the past of another dimension was something completely different.

Throughout his life he had never been involved with organized religion, but on this night he needed to pray. He slowly got up, knelt beside the bed and with eyes closed, he took a deep breath trying to relax. He worked to collect his thoughts, searching for what he needed to say. "Dear God, I am asking for your help tomorrow. I, I'm scared shi...., sorry about that. I'm just scared, that's all and I could really use your help. I know you don't owe me anything but I really would like you to be there tomorrow. Ah, Amen."

He got back in bed feeling as if he might have made some kind of connection. With what, he really wasn't sure, but he did feel better expressing his fear. Later, as he finally drifted off to sleep, he remembered what his dad used to say. "God always watches out for fools, drunks, and little children." He was sure he fit in one of those categories.

Chapter Thirty-Seven

By nine o'clock the following morning, Shaw was going over the pre jump phasing data for the third time since arriving at the lab. Just as he was about to get his second cup of coffee from the kitchen, Crawford appeared suddenly at his office door.

"Ah, good morning, Sir, I wasn't expecting you till later on today. Something I can do for you?"

Crawford walked in and closed the office door behind him. "Couldn't sleep last night," he said pulling up a chair that sat in front of Shaw's desk. "Hasn't happened to me in a long time."

Shaw sat down behind his desk, trying hard to read the deep lines in the Director's face, a combination of genuine fear and sadness. "Sir, is everything all right?"

Crawford waved him off. "Yeah," he said with a sigh, looking at the floor. "I guess we have done all we can do to prep Clark for the jump?" he looked up at Shaw. "Haven't we?"

"I believe so. I mean, we can always use more time, but I think we are ready."

Crawford thought for a moment. "You know, I am starting to feel some remorse at putting Clark in this position. I don't think he saw any other way out."

Shaw could see that the Director was having a real emotional struggle about the jump, something he had never witnessed before. It was both touching and deeply unsettling at the same time.
"Sir, if you want me to postpone the jump, I will. We can..."

"No, stick to the time line," interrupted Crawford standing. "Just make sure we cross all the tees on this one, okay? I think we owe him that much."

Shaw nodded. "Of course, Sir. He will have our best effort. Are you sure there is nothing I can do for you?"

The Director turned around and opened the door to the office. "Just do your job, Doctor," he said walking out into the hallway. "That will be sufficient."

He was still sitting behind his desk trying to get his head around what had just happened when Phillip Crane walked in carrying a thick folder. "Hey, good, you're here. Listen, I just took a full series of scans on the plasma readouts and everything is consistent with a steady proton bleed. The thing that concerns me the most is that there are no geographic coordinates on the grid to lock on to. There is no telling where Clark is going to come down, hopefully not in the middle of some large body of water. I mean really, Hammond, are we gonna send this guy on a blind shot?"

Shaw shook his head. "I'm not calling the tune here, Phil. When the shot callers say jump, all we say is how high. You know that."

Crane set the folder on the desk. "You know, losing Hauser and Campbell brings the body count to forty three." He turned to leave. "But who's counting, right?"

By eight thirty that evening Clark had been fitted with all of the gear he needed to take. Fifty thousand dollars in gold coins had been sewn into the lining of his coat, along with several silk topographical maps, a forty-five caliber Sig Saur pistol with fifty rounds, his chest pack containing the Medallions and the extra laser designator return device. Wearing a pair of green tactical pants and desert combat boots, he resembled any one of the countless military operators currently working all over the Middle East. As an extra precaution, he had been given an emergency flotation belt that could be activated if he had the misfortune of landing in deep water. Landing in the middle of a fourth dimension ocean was something just too terrible to think about.

By quarter to ten, he had started walking down the long hallway to the phasing room. Shaw was at his side going over the last minute checklist. "Okay, remember, stay in a tight tucked position until you stop moving. Keep your mouth guard in and your goggles on. You're going to feel a tremendous blast of frigid air followed by a terrific sense of motion and speed. Okay?"

Clark gave thumbs up. "Got it, Doc."

Shaw pushed open the Phasing room door and followed Clark inside. "And remember, we talked about the intense motion sickness a lot of the guys feel when they land. It's perfectly normal. Throw up. Drink water. Do what you need to do. It will go away within the hour. All right?"

Before Clark could answer, Crawford walked in with several others. "Evening, Agent," announced Crawford. "I can see that you are just about ready to go. Do you have everything you need?"

Clark nodded. "Yeah, good to go."

Shaw tapped him on the shoulder. "Okay, remember the game plan. Stay as long as you feel comfortable, but as soon as you land, send back a shot from the designator so we can get a fix on your position."
Clark smiled, looking at the faces of the men in the room. Every one of them looked like they were about to pass out. "C'mon, guys, lighten up."

Shaw managed a nervous laugh. "Are you ready, Dave?"

Clark looked around the room one last time and then stepped over to the array panels. "Let's go. I'm getting hot in this jacket." With his gut feeling as if he needed to take a six-pound shit, he placed the goggles over his eyes and squatted down on the floor, wrapping his arms tight around his knees.

Shaw nodded to the array panel operator in the glass-enclosed booth to go ahead and fire the board. Instantly the room lit up with a brilliant blue white flash, followed by a deep booming thud that reverberated throughout the building like a million pound ball of iron dropped to earth a mile away.

Shaw slowly walked over to the phasing site, hoping to God he wouldn't see carbonized flesh and bone, a definitive sign of a power overload. It had happened before.

The site was clean. Clark had jumped...

Epilogue:

<u>Yesterday</u>

The old lady had died two weeks ago; leaving a run down house, an overgrown yard, and room after room of neatly stacked cardboard boxes filled with the flotsam of life. In three years, he had spoken or at least waved to her almost everyday. Aside from talking to him, she had kept to herself, her husband long since dead, her children and grand children scattered like seeds across the country from Maine to Nebraska.

Rarely had anyone visited. Most of the time when the Michigan weather was fair, he would sit with her on her back porch in her faded blue Adirondack chairs drinking club soda while looking at the lake. She would talk about the old times, of years gone by when the house was full of the loud happy chaos of family and friends. *"They're all gone now,"* she would say softly, her pale blues eyes tearing. The conversation would pause, the emotion in the air stopping the words.

He had rented the small duplex next door with the intention of only staying the summer. That was four years ago. He had been living in Chicago, working as a technical writer for a software firm, a gig that was a six day a week, nine to five enema that paid six figures but had cost him his marriage and almost his sanity.

When he really allowed himself to think back to those days, he was surprised Bonnie had stayed with him as long as she had. Four years is a long time to survive on nothing but bullshit and heartache. The booze, the late nights, and then the indifference to her needs, finally drove it all over the edge and she had left, no loud tearful fight, no shouted accusations and slamming doors, just a quiet ending and a deep wound that he thought would never heal. Needing a place to go, he had driven the hundred miles to Saint Joseph and rented the first place he found that was near the water. Two weeks later he had quit his job, cashed in his 401 K, and planted an emotional flag in a town he had never even been in before.

He was now making a decent living as a remote medical coder, a job that paid the bills and allowed him to work from his kitchen where he had a stunning view of Lake Michigan less than a hundred yards away. The job allowed him time to write, a passion he'd had even as a kid. Short stories, poems, and several attempts at screenplays filled hundreds of notebooks and boxes with things that nobody would ever read.

Three days after the old woman passed, a local attorney showed up at his door. He introduced himself and then dropped a lightning bolt. The old woman had amended her will just before she died, and he was now the new owner of everything she had owned, house, land, everything. The attorney dropped a key to the front door of her house on the table, a copy of the will, and a bill for two hundred and sixteen dollars, all the while mumbling something about clients with dementia not being allowed to make legal decisions, ever!

The next day he got up early and decided that he would head over and see just how the old woman had been living all these years, having not seen the inside of the house the entire time he lived next door. Walking up on the back porch, he unlocked the back door and stepped inside. The house had that familiar smell of old age and mothballs, the universal fragrance of grandma's house - the mixture of a thousand bacon and egg breakfasts, oceans of strong coffee, and clouds of cheap spray air freshener. It was the smell of home.
After opening the drapes, he quietly walked room to room, noticing the neatly made beds, the clean floors and the

hundreds of carefully stacked cardboard boxes in nearly every room. Upon closer inspection, he discovered that most of the boxes contained books, magazines, and newspapers that dated back to the fifties. He spent days going through the stuff she had collected throwing out hundreds of pounds of old magazines and donating hundreds of books to the local library.

The jewelry, he gave to Good Will along with the few clothes that hung neatly in her closet. After two weeks of work, he had most of the things cleared out and was getting down to several small dressers and boxes stored on the top shelves of closets.

Looking back, he remembered the day he found the envelope. It had been in the bottom left drawer of her dresser, sitting under a large leather bound family Bible. He remembered how shocked he had been to see the six orange and cream-colored Nazi Germany postage stamps on the envelope. He sat down on the bed and read the names that had been written in black ink.

"To: Mrs., Irene Hauser, 727 Haven Street, Saint Joseph, Michigan, USA"
"From: J, Hauser, Munich Germany"

According to the postmark, it had been mailed in the fall of 1939. After reading the astonishing contents of the envelope, he knew what his next novel would be about... and the title was a given: *NOBLE SHADOWS*...... one hell of a story.

The End

Author's footnote:

In November of 2015, while getting the artwork for this novel, an older gentleman standing in line at Staples spoke up when he saw the large promotional sign for the book -the orange and cream Nazi stamp. He said he had been a child living in Poland during the war and had that same stamp in his private collection. While looking at the promotion board you could see his mind transported back in time. Time travel is real. I saw it in the old man's eyes....

Acknowledgements

I wish to make a special dedication to Terri and Linda for their hard work in this endeavor. It could not be done without them.

Made in the USA
Columbia, SC
27 March 2018